"Time-Out's in labor!"

Jessie and Time-Out went way back, and now her favorite horse was going to be a mama! Jessie had been leasing the mare from the owners until they decided to breed her. Now, after all the long months of waiting, Time-Out's foal was on the way. The mare would be a wonderful mother—Jessie was sure of that. And soon, Jessie would be able to ride Time-Out again. That is, if the owners agreed. Jessie wanted it too much to think of anything else.

She began to smile. Having a new colt on the farm would be wonderful. The future was definitely looking up. And if she didn't hurry, she might miss one of the great moments in life.

Quietly, Jessie slipped into the barn. In the foaling box she could hear Time-Out pacing, making deep grunting noises.

Then, all of a sudden, it got very quiet in the barn. At first Jessie wasn't sure why. Then she realized Time-Out's pacing had stopped.

She looked in the stall and saw that the horse was down in the straw, her neck and head stretched out—and the foal was just beginning to emerge. All the fear and anxiety that had tightened Jessie's insides for the last hour turned into something else. Something she had no name for. Something that made her heart swell and want to sing.

"It's born," she said simply.

Other Fawcett Girls Only Titles:

BLUE RIBBON #2
A HORSE OF HER OWN

Chris St. John

FAWCETT GIRLS ONLY • NEW YORK

RLI $\dfrac{\text{VL 5 \& up}}{\text{IL 6 \& up}}$

A Fawcett Girls Only Book
Published by Ballantine Books
Copyright © 1989 by Cloverdale Press, Inc.

Library of Congress Catalog Card Number: 88-92919

ISBN 0-449-13451-2

Manufactured in the United States of America

First Edition: May 1989

Chapter 1

JESSIE ROBESON raced out of the barn. She slid to a stop at the gate that opened into the field between the Windcroft Stables and the Connecticut woods beyond. It was late afternoon, and the tops of the trees looked golden in the slanting rays of the spring sun. Jessie stared toward the tree line, her hazel eyes intent, her brown hair blowing in the breeze. She was trying to see if there was any sign of Kate Wiley or Dara Cooper, her two best friends. But she picked up no movement of any kind.

"Oh," she said aloud, "Kate, where are you?"

The answer to that was, out on the trails. Kate and Dara had taken their horses, Night Owl and Arpeggio, deep into the quiet Connecticut woods. And Jessie would have been with them if she hadn't been so late getting to the farm.

She glanced toward the farmhouse where Kate lived. It was hard to tell if anyone was home. Kate's mother, Anne Wiley, was probably resting inside. It had only been a few weeks since Anne had undergone a knee operation to repair an old riding injury, and she was still taking things easy.

Then Jessie noticed that the Wileys' car wasn't parked in its usual place. Suddenly she remembered that Kate had said something about her mother and father going to some kind of horse-equipment show in Hartford. There didn't seem to be a soul on the farm but Jessie, if you didn't count the horses and a nest of noisy robins in the maple tree.

"What a time to be the only person here," Jessie moaned.

"Maybe I didn't see what I think I saw." She tried to reassure herself. "I *have* been known to jump to conclusions." She turned and faced the barn again, tucking a strand of flyaway hair behind her ear. Her hazel eyes were anxious, her delicate, precise features tight with concern.

There were probably a dozen reasons why Time-Out was acting the way she was, Jessie told herself, trying to stay calm. Name one! her nervous mind demanded. Name one reason, other than labor, that would make a pregnant mare pace around the big stall they had put her in—going in slow circles, dragging her feet through the hay, hanging her head.

That was how Jessie had found Time-Out when she'd arrived a few minutes ago. Kate had said that the mare was acting oddly this morning, but that it was too early for her to be in labor. They had dismissed it as the normal lethargy of a mare well into her pregnancy.

"Good thing you're not a vet, Kate," Jessie muttered, still staring at the barn. Now *think*, she told herself. What had Kate's mother told them about the foaling?

"Mares like privacy," Anne had said. "I've known horses to hold back a birth for hours until they were alone. So if you're around when it happens, keep a low profile. Don't let Time-Out know you're there."

Jessie's heart was pounding in her chest so that she could hardly breathe—partly from excitement for Time-Out and partly from excitement for herself. After long months of waiting, she could finally see the day coming when she'd be able to ride Time-Out again. She had never admitted completely to anyone how much she'd missed that and how she longed for, hoped for, the day to come when Time-Out would be hers to ride once more.

Jessie *had* to see what was happening with the mare now. She tiptoed back into the barn, moving stealthily, and eased herself into the stall next to Time-Out's. She peered through the gap that had been purposely left between the slats separating this stall from the mare's foaling box so that Time-Out could be watched without being disturbed.

Time-Out was pacing restlessly back and forth. There was a fine sheen of perspiration on her neck and withers. Her nostrils were flared, and she was breathing heavily. Suddenly she stopped pacing and swung her head down to prod at her stomach with her nose, as if trying to figure out where all the strange sensations were coming from.

Jessie, utterly terrified, closed her eyes tightly. Please don't let this happen now, she silently begged the mare. I'm only sixteen and not very good at handling crises. Kate and Dara are the ones who know how to take over—and neither of them is here.

A soft sound, like a sigh, pulled Jessie's eyes open again. Time-Out had lain down on the hay. "Oh, no," Jessie whispered frantically. Obviously Time-Out wasn't going to be able to do things Jessie's way.

I've got to do something to make Time-Out more comfortable, Jessie thought frantically. But Anne Wiley had told her not to interfere if she was around for the birth!

What if something went wrong, though. What if something happened to Time-Out—something she, Jessie, could have prevented if she'd helped?

Jessie backed slowly out of the stall and forced herself to move quietly as an Indian until she reached the outside. She gave one last frantic look toward the trails, but there was no sign of the girls. Then, throwing caution to the wind, she took off at a dead run for the house. Let the door be open! Let the door be open! she repeated to herself over and over. She took the few steps to the back door in one leap, reached for the door-knob, and almost fainted with relief when the door opened.

She tripped over the rug in front of the sink on her way to the telephone and kept her balance only by grabbing the back of a chair. She had barely steadied herself when Anne Wiley called from the den, "Kate? Is that you?"

"Mrs. Wiley!" Jessie's voice was breathless with relief. "You're home! I thought you went to Hartford."

"Mr. Wiley went without me. Jessie, what's the matter?"

Jessie ran into the den. Anne Wiley was lying on the couch, looking worried. "Where's Kate?" Anne asked immediately.

"I don't know," Jessie said—and Mrs. Wiley turned pale. "No! I didn't mean that the way it sounded!" Jessie exclaimed. "Kate's fine. She's out on the trails with Dara. That's not the trouble. It's Time-Out. I think she's having her foal!"

Quickly she described the mare's behavior. Anne Wiley listened closely and smiled. "Sure sounds like it to me," she said.

How can she be so relaxed? Jessie wondered. "Shouldn't we be doing something?" she asked frantically.

"Jessie," Mrs. Wiley said quietly, "we should calm down. Time-Out will be fine. She knows exactly what she's doing."

"But shouldn't we call the vet?"

"It's a little early for that. These things take time. We probably should call the Jespers, though. Why don't you do that for me? In the meantime, I'll get myself up on these crutches and start for the barn. It'll probably take an hour, the way I move these days."

"Should I boil some water?" Jessie asked. It was a question she'd heard a lot of times in the movies. She'd never been able to figure out what the water was for.

"Good idea," Mrs. Wiley said on her way out the door. "A cup of tea will relax us both."

"Tea?" Jessie said, puzzled.

"It was just a joke," Anne answered, and smiled.

"Forget the water, Jessie. Make the call and meet me in the barn."

Anne Wiley made her way slowly out of the house, and Jessie dashed to the telephone. The Jespers' telephone number was written on the blackboard next to it. She dialed Time-Out's owner's number, jiggling her foot with impatience as the phone rang. It took four rings before Mrs. Jesper answered.

"Mrs. Jessie, this is Jesper Robeson—no, wait— let me start again. It's Jessie, Mrs. Jesper. I'm at Windcroft. We think Time-Out's in labor!"

"Oh, really?" Mrs. Jesper said excitedly. "When did she start?"

"I'm not sure. Maybe half an hour ago," Jessie said.

"We've got time, then. I'll be there as quickly as I can. Thanks, Jessie. This is a big day for us, isn't it?"

"Yes," Jessie said, and hung up the phone.

Suddenly she felt as if all her strength had leaked out through her feet. If she didn't sit down, she would fall down. She eased herself into one of the kitchen chairs and took a deep breath.

Jessie and Time-Out went way back. She'd been leasing the mare from the Jespers until they decided to breed her. What a terrible disappointment it had been when Mrs. Jesper had told Jessie that she wouldn't be able to ride Time-Out again!

All of last year Jessie had been without a horse. The Wileys had been wonderful, though. They'd given her the chance to ride as often as they could. When Anne Wiley had had her operation, she'd even lent Jessie her horse, Jonathan, to ride until Anne's knee was healed.

Jonathan was a great horse, but he just wasn't

Time-Out. Jessie would have been hard put to explain just what the connection was between her and the gentle mare, but whatever it was, it was strong and lasting. Maybe it had its roots in the fact that during the hard times after Jessie's mother's death two years ago, it had been Time-Out who had given Jessie something to look forward to. It was Time-Out who had taken a grief-stricken Jessie out onto the trails in the healing quiet of the woods and let her cry until there were no more tears. Somehow Jessie felt that Time-Out really understood her. They were more than horse and rider, they were friends.

And now, after all the long months of waiting, Time-Out's foal was on the way. The mare would be a wonderful mother—Jessie was sure of that. And then, after the foal was weaned, Mrs. Jesper would lease Time-Out to Jessie again. She hadn't actually said she would, but Jessie was sure it was going to happen. She wanted it too much to think of anything else.

Jessie began to smile. Having a new baby on the farm would be wonderful. As a matter of fact, now that things seemed to be under control, everything was wonderful. The future was definitely looking up. And if she didn't hurry, she might miss one of the great moments in life.

Anne Wiley was sitting quietly on a hay bale in the stall next to Time-Out—a pile of towels in her lap, her crutches on the floor beside her. She smiled and put her finger to her lips when she saw Jessie. Quietly, Jessie slipped in next to her.

In the foaling box she could hear Time-Out pacing again, making deep grunting noises. She sat down next to Anne, prepared for a long wait.

"I called the vet," Anne whispered. "Time-Out's further along than I thought, and I left a note for Kate on the barn door so she won't come in like her usual cyclone."

Jessie grinned. Cyclone was a good description for Kate. "She's going to miss the whole thing," Jessie whispered.

Anne nodded and smiled.

It was suddenly very quiet in the barn. At first Jessie wasn't sure why. Then she realized Time-Out's pacing had stopped. She looked nervously at Anne, and Anne motioned to her to look through the gap into the foal box.

Time-Out was down in the straw, her neck and head stretched out—and the foal was just beginning to emerge. All the fear and anxiety that had tightened Jessie's insides for the last hour turned into something else. Something she had no name for. Something that made her heart swell and want to sing.

Two small pink hooves were suddenly visible, then a minute pink nose. And then—as smoothly and silently as if the tiny animal were slipping down a slide—the entire foal emerged and lay on the straw next to its mother.

"What's happening?" Anne Wiley asked in a strained whisper, reaching for her crutches.

Jessie turned to Anne, her face bright with wonder. She tried twice before she could get the words out.

"It's born," she said simply.

"Oh, my goodness! That was quick!" Anne struggled to her feet and made her way to the viewing gap. Time-Out was lying quietly, her breathing deep and regular.

"We'll have to wipe the membrane off the foal to make sure it can breathe easily," Anne said. "That'll give Time-Out a minute to relax. Here, take these towels." She handed Jessie the pile of soft white terry. "Go in quietly and talk to her, then rub the foal down as gently as you can."

"Me?" Jessie squeaked.

"Certainly not me," Anne Wiley said, "not on these crutches. The poor thing would have a heart attack, and Time-Out would have a stroke. Besides, Time-Out knows you better then she knows me."

Better than she knows anybody, Jessie thought to herself as she took the towels and approached the foaling box. Time-Out made a soft sound deep in her chest when she saw Jessie. "Hi, sweetie," Jessie said. "You're a mother now, and your baby's beautiful."

Jessie knelt down beside the little animal and moved the soft towels gently over the fragile shoulders and sharply angled hocks. "He's a colt," she said softly to Anne, who was standing at the door to the foaling box now.

As they watched, the colt struggled to his feet and stood, bobbing like a punch-drunk fighter. "Oh, look at him," Jessie said with a ragged breath. The little animal gave a nervous bleat. Time-Out raised her head, flicking her ears forward. The colt peered at Jessie, blinking solemnly as if trying to determine who she was.

"No," Jessie said. The word was halfway between a laugh and a sob. "I'm not your mother. That's your mother over there!"

As if on cue, Time-Out lurched to her feet, stood for a minute to gain her equilibrium, and then turned to nose the small, shaky bundle. She ran her tongue tentatively along his miniature flanks. Then, gathering assurance, she swiped the colt's shoulders. The strength of Time-Out's lick sent the colt sprawling, and this time Jessie did laugh.

The mare looked at Jessie with puzzled eyes as if to say, "What am I doing wrong?"

"Try it again," Jessie urged, "but easier." Jessie stood up and backed out of the stall just in time to see Dr. Rosen, the vet, coming quietly into the barn.

"You're too late for the big event," Anne said, and smiled.

The vet came to stand beside them and peer into the box. "I'm usually just a bystander at these things anyway," he said. "But as long as I'm here, I might as well earn my fee and give the colt his tetanus shot."

Jessie and Anne watched while he checked both horses and proclaimed them in excellent health. The colt was standing now and nursing noisily. Time-Out stared at her audience, her dark eyes calm and happy.

"I think we should give them some privacy," Anne said.

"That's about all they're going to need for a while," Dr. Rosen agreed.

Jessie lingered. She wanted to make sure the picture of Time-Out and her colt was imprinted on her memory, to be sure she would carry the memory of this moment with her forever. After a long minute, she followed Anne and the vet out of the barn.

As Dr. Rosen went over the care and handling

of the colt with Anne, Jessie walked to the fence and climbed up on the top rail. Excitement was bubbling inside her. What a wonderful thing she had seen! Maybe the closest thing to a miracle she'd ever witness!

Just then a movement off in the distance caught her eye. Jessie looked closer. It was Kate and Night Owl trotting out of the woods. Jessie waited until Kate was close enough to see her, then stood on the bottom rail and waved frantically. Night Owl switched from a trot to a full gallop, and in a matter of minutes Kate was reining to a stop in front of Jessie.

"I waited forever for you guys!" Kate said.

"I know. I got held up. Dara didn't come either?" Kate shook her head. "You will never in a million years guess what happened this afternoon," Jessie went on. Kate's blue-gray eyes searched her friend's face. "Time-Out had her foal!" Jessie said triumphantly.

"No!" Kate wailed, standing up in the stirrups. She looked toward the barn and saw her mother talking to Dr. Rosen. "No," she said again, despondently sitting back in the saddle. "I missed the whole thing?"

"The whole thing," Jessie said.

"Did you see it?"

"It was wonderful. It's a colt. The Jespers weren't even here."

That knowledge sent a warm little rush through Jessie. It almost made Time-Out and the new colt seem more hers and less theirs. In Jessie's daydreams Time-Out belonged to her. It was always a shock when she remembered the Jespers.

A scrunch of wheels on the driveway announced

Mrs. Jesper's arrival. She got out of the car and walked quickly over to Anne Wiley and the vet. Kate dismounted, and she and Jessie joined the group.

Mrs. Jesper was laughing. "She's a cagey little thing," she was saying. "I came to see her this morning. I thought she was acting funny, but not that funny. She certainly can keep a secret."

I'd have known, Jessie thought. If I'd seen her this morning, I'd have known.

"Can I go in to see them?" Mrs. Jesper asked Dr. Rosen.

"Me, too?" Kate asked, handing Night Owl's reins to Jessie.

"Just for a minute," the vet said, and they rushed toward the barn.

When they came out, Mrs. Jesper was delighted. "His markings are just like the stallion's, and his conformation looks wonderful. Of course it's a little early to tell. But if he turns out as well as his daddy, he'll be one wonderful horse."

If he turns out to be as nice as his mother, Jessie thought, he'll be even more wonderful, and she smiled broadly at the thought.

"She's a good broodmare," Dr. Rosen said. "Will you breed her again?"

Jessie's smile froze on her lips. What did he mean? She looked anxiously from Dr. Rosen to Mrs. Jesper. It had never occurred to her that the Jespers might breed Time-Out again! She waited, barely breathing, for Mrs. Jesper's answer—and when it came, it was devastating.

"I'm not sure," Mrs. Jesper said. "We're going to be moving at the end of the summer. We may breed her, or we may sell her, or we may just take her with us. We haven't decided yet."

The words dropped like ice into Jessie's brain. Time-Out *leaving*? Mrs. Jesper was talking about the mare as if she were a sack of meal with no feelings at all! No matter which one of the choices Mrs. Jesper decided on, Time-Out would be miserable—Jessie was sure of it. And no matter what choice she picked, there wasn't a chance in the world that Time-Out would be Jessie's to ride again.

No one had noticed Jessie's shock.

"Well, I guess I'll be on my way," Dr. Rosen said. "I'll stop by tomorrow to give them another look, but I'm sure everything will be fine."

"Thanks," Mrs. Jesper said. "And thank you, too," she said, and included Jessie and Anne in her smile. "Now all we have to do is settle on a name for him."

Kate took Night Owl's reins back from Jessie and led him to the barn. "Want to help me untack?" she asked.

Jessie, stupefied, just stared at her friend as if Kate were speaking a foreign language. "What? Oh, no. I've got to get home," she said slowly.

"Are you okay?" Kate asked. "You look a little weird."

"Sure," Jessie said, and forced a smile. "It's just been an exciting few hours."

"Wait until Dara hears! She sure picked the wrong day to go to the dentist," Kate prattled happily. "See you tomorrow!" She waved and walked toward the barn.

Jessie stayed where she was for a minute. Then she shook her head. "How can you be this upset?" she asked herself. "Time-Out isn't yours. She never was yours. The Jespers can do anything they want with her. You know that."

But knowing it and accepting it were two different things. Good thing Jessie hadn't let Kate in on her plans for the future—plans that were nothing more than pipe dreams now.

I should have known this was the way it would go, Jessie thought bitterly. For the last few years, the only luck she'd had had been bad. What in the world had made her think that Mrs. Jesper would care enough about Jessie to consider her feelings?

You are the biggest dope in the entire state of Connecticut, she told herself, savagely picking up her bicycle.

Jessie pedaled home at such a furious pace that she covered the distance between Windcroft and her home in half the time it usually took. By the time she'd gotten her breath back and stowed her bike in the garage, she had calmed herself down.

In the kitchen Mrs. McPhaden, the Robesons' housekeeper, was peering anxiously into the oven. "Hello there, Jessie," she said over her shoulder. "Five more minutes until dinner. How were things at the farm?"

"You'll never guess what happened today," Jessie said, trying to sound excited.

"Jessie's home, Jessie's home!" Her eight-year-old sister's piping voice floated into the kitchen from the hallway, followed almost immediately by its owner. Sarah Robeson ran to Jessie and hugged her hard.

Jessie reached down to hug Sarah back, fighting down an unreasonable desire to cry. She held on tightly to the little girl until she'd regained her composure.

"So what's the big news?" Mrs. McPhaden asked.

Jessie backed far enough away from Sarah so that she could see the little girl's face. "Time-Out had her foal today." She made her voice bright, and Sarah's face lit up with excitement.

"Tell me!" Sarah demanded. And Jessie did, making the afternoon sound perfectly wonderful.

Chapter 2

A horn honked loudly in the Robesons' drive. Nick Robeson, Jessie's ten-year-old brother, stuck his head in the front door and called, "Jessie, Dara and Kate are here." Then he raced back outside, slamming the door after him.

Mr. Robeson, who was reading the paper in the living room, looked up at his oldest daughter. "Where are you headed?" he asked.

"To the mall," Jessie said.

"Can I come?" Sarah asked.

"And leave me all alone?" her father said in mock alarm. "Who would I read *Winnie-the-Pooh* with if you go out?"

"Okay." Sarah had a pleased smile on her face. "I'll stay home."

"Thanks," Jessie said, and grinned at her father.

"Not too late," Mr. Robeson warned. "And tell Nick he's got five more minutes to make a home run before he has to come in."

Jessie pulled on an oversized gray sweatshirt,

fluffed up her shoulder-length brown hair, and stepped out into the spring twilight. It was so nice to feel the warm air against her face instead of the icy cold of a New England winter! She passed her father's message along to her brother, who was playing street baseball with the neighborhood kids. "No way!" he protested. But Jessie just ignored him and climbed into the small red car Dara had gotten when she received her driver's license.

Kate was sitting in the front seat. She smiled a hello as Jessie closed the car door.

"Don't run over the outfield," Jessie said as Dara backed down the driveway.

"Did he make Little League All-Stars?" Kate asked as they watched Nick take some practice swings over the doormat that served as home plate.

"We're waiting to hear," Jessie said.

"I thought only girls spent their time waiting to hear," Dara said. Her short blond hair swung out in a shining arc as she turned to face front again.

"What are we waiting for now?" Jessie asked.

"What are we always waiting for? A phone call."

"From whom?"

Kate turned to face Jessie. "This afternoon, in study hall, Doug Lyons sat with Dara. The last thing he told her was, 'I'll give you a call later.' Can you believe it?"

Jessie bounced in her seat with excitement. "Then what in heaven's name are you doing in this car on the way to the mall? Why aren't you home chained to the telephone?" she asked.

Doug Lyons was probably the best-looking boy in school, not to mention that he was co-captain of the football team and president of the junior class. He was as handsome as Dara was beautiful. Together, they'd be an incredible couple.

"Because then it would look as if I cared whether he called or not," Dara said offhandedly.

"Don't you?" Jessie asked, astonished.

"Of course I do," Dara said. Her deep blue eyes met Jessie's hazel ones in the rearview mirror. "But I'm not going to let *him* know that. When I'm not home tonight, he'll call tomorrow."

And he would. Jessie was sure of it. Things always happened the right way for people like Dara—people who were pretty and nice and smart and sure of themselves. She glanced over at Kate. Kate was shaking her head and laughing at Dara's cool assurance—but in a lot of ways Kate was like Dara. There were things in life both girls wanted, and they seemed able to plan ahead and make them happen. In her life, Jessie felt, it was just the opposite. Want something too much and you could be sure you *wouldn't* get it.

Jessie was finding it harder and harder these days to feel happy. It was as though she constantly carried a chip on her shoulder. Every time Kate or Dara said something funny, Jessie would laugh—but inside she was saying, "Sure, you guys can joke. You've got things pretty much the way you want them."

Kate's mom and dad owned Windcroft Stables, and Kate had a super horse, Night Owl, that was her very own. Dara's parents were rich enough that they had been able to afford to buy her a horse, Arpeggio, who was every bit as good as the Owl. Kate and Dara were probably the best three-day-event riders in Connecticut. They kept telling

Jessie she'd be just as good if she rode as much as they did.

Only to ride you had to have a horse. Jessie had been coming along nicely on Time-Out. She wasn't making the fantastic progress that Kate and Night Owl were making. She wasn't winning blue ribbons in competition after competition the way Kate was. But Kate had her heart set on getting to the Olympics someday. All Jessie had her heart set on was Time-Out.

Jessie sighed as she watched the scenery change out the car window. Why was having a horse of her own so important to her? Lots of girls never thought about horses at all!

Kate and Dara certainly weren't thinking about them now. In the front seat Kate was talking about having her hair trimmed. "Just the ends, to kind of even them out," she said.

"I'll do that for you," Dara said. "If you go to a beauty parlor, they'll take inches off."

"And that's not what I want," Kate said, running her hand along the blond hair that reached halfway down her back. "Long hair's not in style anymore. My dad calls me the last of the flower children. But I don't care. I've had it for ages, and I can't stand the thought of cutting it. Besides, it looks so classy pulled back in a bun or a braid when I event."

Dara pulled into the mall lot and parked. "And what's more important, looking good in school or in the eventing ring?" she asked as she switched off the engine. It was a question that did not require an answer.

Once the girls were inside the mall, Jessie's spirits rose a little. She liked the excitement she felt here. It was almost like the few times she'd gone to Hartford or New York. All the people and the noise lifted her spirits.

They headed immediately for the ice-cream shop and slid into a booth. Amory Baxter, a friend from school who worked at the shop, gave them a friendly wave. In a minute he was at their table to take their order.

The three girls didn't need to look at the menu. "Three hot fudge sundaes, buttercrunch ice-cream and double whipped cream," Dara said.

"Don't you three get tired of ordering the same thing all the time?" Amory asked, his eyes on Jessie. He glanced over his shoulder at the big menu hanging above the counter. "We have twenty-seven flavors of ice cream that you've never even sampled."

"When we're ready to take the big step to a new flavor, you'll be the first to know," Dara said.

"Boring," Amory muttered, walking away.

"We are not!" Kate said after him. She sat up a little to look around the store.

"He's not here," Dara said, and grinned when Kate blushed.

"Pete Hastings?" Jessie asked, and Kate nodded.

"Did you think he would be?" asked Jessie. "I wish you two would go out and get it over with. It's going to be an anticlimax when it finally happens."

"It sort of set us back a little when I had to break that date we made right after the three-day eventing competition at The Hill. I think Pete's afraid I might do that again. So we're working up to it," Kate told her. "Slowly," she added.

"Some people get engaged and married in less

time than it's taking you and Pete to get around to a date. How many times has he called you?" Jessie asked.

"I've stopped counting," Kate said.

"You're right. He probably *is* afraid you're going to say no again. Maybe you're going to have to get the ball rolling and ask *him* out," Dara put in.

"How does that fit in with your theory of not looking anxious?" Kate asked her.

"Oh, with you and Pete it doesn't matter. Everybody knows he's crazy about you."

"Do they?" Kate had a delighted smile on her face.

"Sure. Call him up tomorrow and ask him to go to the movies," Dara urged. "We're liberated now. We can do the inviting just as easily as the guys can!"

For a second Kate looked as if she were thinking the idea over. Then she said reluctantly, "I couldn't, even if I wanted to. I'm going to be busy all day tomorrow—and so will you two, if you agree to help."

Amory plopped three gooey sundaes down in front of them before Jessie could ask, "Help with what?"

"Enjoy," he said.

"I think he likes you," Kate told Jessie when Amory had gone.

"Who? Amory?" Jessie asked. "Are you *crazy*?"

"I mean it. You know today, when you didn't show up for lunch? I thought he was going to go into an anxiety attack right in front of us. And did you catch the way he looked at her just now?" Kate asked Dara.

"Uh-huh." Dara said. "It was amazing. He used both eyes!"

"Laugh if you want to, you guys, but I'll bet I'm right." Kate spooned a big blob of whipped cream into her mouth and closed her eyes in bliss. "Right after horses, God made whipped cream and hot fudge," she said.

Jessie looked over to where Amory was stacking glasses. He had his back to her. If what Kate said was true, shouldn't she have felt some vibes? It probably *wasn't* true. It was just Kate wanting to arrange things for Jessie. Dara had Doug, Kate had Pete, so Jessie had to have Amory. Jessie decided to put the whole thing out of her mind.

They were halfway through the sundaes before Dara thought to ask again, "What do you want us to do on Saturday?"

"Oh, yeah. You both know that Mr. Yon is closing up his stables, right?" Kate asked.

The girls nodded. Pietro Yon was a family friend of the Wileys'. In fact, he had been Anne Wiley's coach when she was still riding. He had a wonderful reputation, and Mrs. Cooper, Dara's mother, had hoped to get him to coach Dara when the Coopers moved to Smithfield a few months ago. But on doctor's orders, Mr. Yon was retiring and moving to Florida.

"Well, he needs some help cleaning out the barns and attics and places," Kate told them. "Mom said we'd go, and I thought you guys might want to come. He's going to be getting rid of a lot of stuff—maybe we can pick up some tack."

"What did he do with his horses?" Dara asked.

"Sold them. Last I heard he only had one left, Northern Spy. He's so funny about his horses. He treats them as though they were his children. Mom says he's had a dozen people come to look at Spy and he's found a reason not to sell to any of them. He says they aren't good enough to own him."

"Is he going to keep him?" Dara asked.

"No," Kate said. "But I think he's hoping to keep him in the family at least. Mrs. Yon's sister-in-law is coming from Virginia to see him tomorrow. My mom says Mrs. Yon's brother is some bigwig lawyer in Washington. So they have the money to keep the horse in the way Mr. Yon wants him kept ... if they like him. So do you guys want to come?"

"I'm game," Dara said. "Arpeggio could use a day of rest, and I haven't got anything else to do."

"It'll be fun," Kate said. "Mr. Yon's house is almost as old as our house is."

"Does his house have a ghost, too?" Jessie asked.

"Does *your* house have a ghost?" Dara stared at Kate, her eyes wide.

"I don't know, is the answer to your question," Kate said to Jessie. "And we're not sure, is the answer to your question," she said to Dara.

"What time do we have to be there?" Dara asked.

"Be at my house at eight," Kate told her.

"What about Doug Lyons?" Jessie asked, spooning up the last of her sundae.

Dara pursed her lips as she considered the question. "If he called tonight and I wasn't home and he calls tomorrow and I'm not home, I'll call him."

"And if you call him," Kate said, "I'll call Pete, and Jessie can call Amory."

"I will not," Jessie said. Kate paid no attention.

"A done deal," Dara said, holding out her hand for Kate to slap. "Do you want me to pick you up tomorrow?" she asked Jessie.

"I didn't say I would come," Jessie said.

"Of course you'll come," Kate said.

"Of course I'll come," Jessie said after a second, wondering if Kate would hear the hint of sarcasm in her voice.

Chapter 3

JESSIE folded the last of the horse blankets and put them inside a cardboard carton. How could anyone, even anyone as old as Mr. Yon, accumulate so much stuff? She taped the flaps down and labeled the box in big black letters. Dara was working in one of the utility sheds with her, going through a maze of bridles and reins to pick out the ones worth keeping.

"Did you ever see so many bridles?" Jessie asked, sitting down for a minute on the box she had just sealed.

"Some of these things look about a hundred years old. He must have brought them with him from Europe," Dara said. "Didn't Kate say he did some work with the Lippizaners?"

"I think so. He's a neat old man, isn't he?" Jessie said.

"He sure is. I wish he had stayed in the business a little longer," Dara said. "I'd have liked to have had him for my coach."

"You'll love having Kate's mom coach you," Jessie told her, "once she's back on her feet again. She knows so much about riding. And look how much she's taught Kate."

"I'll love having Kate's mom," Dara agreed, "but my mother's going to take some convincing. She's a real snob about some things," Dara said, shaking her head.

"I've never known anyone who has the kind of relationship with her mother that you do," Jessie said with a sidelong glance at Dara.

"You mean because we're always arguing?" Dara said, and smiled. "Mom's not as difficult as you may think. Most of our differences are about my riding—and the only time you get to see her is around horses, when she's at the barn or a competition.

"She thinks that all you have to do is spend a lot of money and you automatically get the best," Dara went on. "Maybe that's true for clothes and houses, but it isn't always true about riding. The fact is that I know more about riding and horses than my mother does, and when she's wrong, I have to tell her. After all, I'm the one doing the riding, not her. And once she's had time to think things over, she usually agrees that I was right." Dara ran a hand down an especially beautiful bridle. "This leather is like silk," she said appreciatively.

"You're really sure enough about your opinions to stand up for them?"

"Sure," Dara said, looking up in surprise. "Wouldn't you?"

"No," Jessie said. "I don't have very strong opinions, I guess."

"Then you ought to get some," Dara said.

Jessie laughed. "Okay. I'll check and see if I can pick up a few at Woolworth's. In the meantime, I'll get this over to the truck. It'll give us a little more room to move around." She shoved the carton she had just packed toward the door.

Outside, the sun was blinding after the dim light in the shed. Jessie didn't even see Pietro Yon until she collided with him.

"Jessie!" he said, holding out his hand to steady her. "Where is Kate?" When she paused, he said again in great agitation, "Where is Kate?"

"I don't know," Jessie said, pausing to put down the box. "Is something wrong?"

Mr. Yon looked at her and then over his shoulder at a cloud of dust that was moving steadily up the driveway toward the farm. He muttered something in a foreign language—and from the tone of his voice, Jessie was sure she shouldn't ask him to translate. Then he stared at her as if he were trying to figure out the size and shape of her brain.

She had no idea if what he saw pleased him. In any case, he grabbed her arm and hurried her toward the barn. "There is no help for it. You will have to rise to the occasion," he informed her.

"What occasion?" Jessie panted, running to keep up with him.

"In that car that is rapidly approaching my barn are a young man and his mother, who is my wife's sister-in-law. She has it in her head that Northern Spy would be a good horse for her son."

"Yes," Jessie agreed, a little breathless from the pace Mr. Yon was setting. "I know. Kate said

someone from your family was coming to see
him. That's great."

"Not everyone—not even if they are family—is
welcome on my horses or in my barns," Mr. Yon
said angrily.

Jessie felt totally confused. "Do you want me to
stop them from coming into the barn?" she asked.
She could just see herself and Mr. Yon armed
with pitchforks, and fending them off.

Mr. Yon stared at her in surprise. "The barn?
What has the barn to do with any of this? No. I
want you on the horse. If they want to see Spy go,
you will show them. Quickly!" he said. "You must
be on him before they arrive. Get him ready. I will
stall them in the paddock. When he's tacked up,
bring him to the exercise ring."

"Me?" Jessie said. "I've never ridden Spy in my
life. I've never even seen him!"

"Then you are in for an experience," Mr. Yon
said, pausing in their headlong flight to smile at
her. "He is a wonder. Now hurry up!" Behind
them Jessie could hear the sound of a car stopping near the house. With a little shove, Mr. Yon
propelled her toward the stalls. Then he turned
to hurry back the way he had come.

"Pietro!" The name was floating down to them
from the parking area. "We're here!"

"Hurray," Jessie heard Mr. Yon mutter sullenly
under his breath as he made his way toward the
car. "Such good news!"

For a moment Jessie hesitated, unsure of what
she should do. At the curve of the path Mr. Yon
turned around. When he saw her still staring after
him, he made a shooing motion with his hands,

urging her into the barn. Sighing, Jessie shrugged and went inside.

The stalls were empty, except for one. In it stood a chestnut gelding with four white stockings. His back was toward the aisle, his head stuck dejectedly into a corner.

As soon as Jessie touched the lock on the stall door, the horse's head came up and his ears pricked forward. "Spy?" she asked nervously. She'd never laid eyes on this horse—and here she was about to attempt to saddle and ride him!

I should have said no to Mr. Yon, she told herself. I should have said, I am having my first opinion, Mr. Yon. And my opinion is that this is a crazy person's assignment. That was what Dara would have done. "But I'm not Dara, am I?" Jessie said aloud to the horse, who was looking over his shoulder at her now. A long white blaze ran from his forelock to his nose.

Spy stared at her unblinking, then snorted. "Okay, so you're not Dara," his eyes seemed to say. "Who are you, and what do you have in mind?"

Jessie pulled open the stall door. Spy turned to face her, reaching out a tentative nose for a good sniff. He inhaled deeply, and sneezed.

"*Gesundheit!*" Jessie said, slowly running a hand along his neck. He stood quietly under her touch. "Well, you look pretty friendly," Jessie said. The words were hopeful. "Are you?" Spy gazed at her impassively. "Okay. Here goes nothing," Jessie said, clipping a lead line to the gelding's halter and securing him in the aisle.

A long slanting ray of sun fell through the open barn door and glistened on Spy's bright chestnut coat. "Oh my," Jessie said stepping back from him. "You *are* a beauty. No wonder Mr. Yon is finding it hard to let you go. Well, there's somebody at the ring to see you, and it's my job to show you off. What do you think of that?"

Spy gazed at her calmly, as if showing off were second nature to him. Jessie brushed him quickly, gave his feet a fast going-over, and then saddled and bridled him. He stood quietly, accepting her attentions, but Jessie had the feeling it was because she was new to him and he was looking her over, too. Somehow she was sure that standing quietly was not one of the things Spy usually did well.

"Now comes the tricky part," Jessie said, leading the glowing animal to the barn door. "Now I get on your back, and you pretend to listen carefully to everything I tell you. And you don't get silly, and you don't make me nervous. Agreed?" Spy stared out into the bright morning and nodded his head up and down, nibbling the bit.

Mr. Yon would certainly never ask me to ride a horse that was dangerous, Jessie assured herself. Taking one deep breath, she placed her foot in the stirrup, hopped twice and pulled herself into the saddle. She felt Spy gather himself under her weight, but he didn't move. "Well, you've got better manners than Time-Out," Jessie said, taking up the reins. "She'd have been halfway up the path by now." Jessie squeezed gently with her legs, and Spy stepped forward. His smooth, long strides brought him to the exercise ring in a matter of seconds.

"Aha," Mr. Yon called out. "Here they are."

Jessie looked over to see a brooding, dark-haired young man watching her with a sour expression on his face. Next to him stood a stocky woman who was examining Jessie and Spy with an intense frown. And next to her stood Mr. Yon, smiling angelically.

He said something to the woman, then called out to Jessie, "Circle him at the trot."

Jessie did as she was told—and felt an electric spark run between her and Spy. A tingling feeling surged from the gelding up through her hands and into her arms. It made her heart skip a beat.

This was nothing like riding Time-Out. When Jessie was on the mare, the two of them had what Jessie called "conference" about what they were going to do next, and some kind of agreement was reached before they did it. But with Spy, the slightest change in her position or in the tension of the reins brought an immediate response. No sooner did a thought occur to Jessie—even if it was something she didn't particularly want to do—than Spy somehow sensed it and made the change.

He was going at a strong, steady trot now. His feet hit the ground with a rhythmical one-two beat. Jessie leaned forward a fraction of an inch, and Spy picked up speed. She gathered in the reins a little, and he came right back to her—slowing, steadying, giving her the impression she had hitched a ride on a wind that was only being obedient for the moment.

Jessie stole a quick glance at the rail and saw that Kate and Anne Wiley had joined the little group. Then she brought her mind right back to what she was doing. This was no time for thinking about anything but what she was doing. All her attention had to be kept completely on Spy and what she was telling him.

The tingle of excitement in her chest increased, her heartbeat accelerated, and a tiny sliver of fear edged its way into Jessie's mind. This was the most difficult riding she'd ever done. She tried not to think about how much control she had to exert to keep Spy at his wonderful, even trot. If she relaxed for even a second, who knew what he might try?

"Jessie!" She turned briefly to look at Mr. Yon. "Canter him," he called.

She nodded once, then focused again on the two sharp ears right in front of her. Praying that Spy wouldn't give her more than she asked for, Jessie squeezed her legs just the barest bit and loosened the tension on his reins. Spy slipped from a trot to a canter so balanced and comfortable that they had gone halfway around the ring before Jessie realized how fast they were going.

"Control! Control!" Mr. Yon called—at just about the same time that Jessie realized she might have lost control.

"I'm willing," she muttered to herself through clenched teeth. "The question is, is he?" What if she couldn't stop him? What if he circled faster and faster until they looked like one of those plastic pinwheels you got at a fair—spinning so rapidly in the slightest breath of wind that the colors blurred?

Jessie pulled back on the reins. She was prepared to *fight* Spy for control, but, to her amazement, Spy came onto the bit and slowed to a trot. As she continued to pull him in, he dropped to a walk and then halted altogether.

Afraid to move, almost afraid to breathe, Jessie looked over at the railing. She was thinking to herself that considering the way she'd been plunked on Spy's back, she hadn't done a half-bad job. She was also hoping that Mr. Yon wouldn't ask her to do more. If she had to get this dynamo moving again, she might not be as lucky as she had been the first time.

The stocky woman at the rail had stopped frowning. Now she was jabbing Mr. Yon with her finger. Then she pointed—first at Jessie and Spy, then at the house, and then at Mr. Yon. She definitely did not look happy.

The whole time she was carrying on, Mr. Yon stood with his head lowered, his eyes on the ground. Once in a while he shrugged and shook his head. Anne Wiley and Kate watched quietly, their faces totally blank.

Finally the young man and the woman began walking toward their car. Even at a distance, Jessie could see that they were furious.

Jessie wished she knew how to faint at will. Obviously she'd made a shambles of things. She had probably ruined Mr. Yon's one chance to keep Spy in the family. And she'd thought she'd done so well!

As everyone watched, the car disappeared down the drive. It left a telltale cloud of dust just over the tops of the newly green trees.

Jessie dismounted dispiritedly and led Spy over to the rail, "I'm so sorry," she said. "I did my best, but he's really a handful."

At the sound of her voice, Mr. Yon, Anne, and Kate all turned to look at her. Mr. Yon was smiling broadly, and Kate was laughing out loud.

"What are you sorry about?" Kate asked her friend. "You rode him like a pro."

"I did?" Jessie said, surprised.

"You did," Anne Wiley agreed. Then she turned to Mr. Yon. "You old fraud," she said, and smiled.

"You do what you have to do," Mr. Yon said with a shrug.

"If I rode him so well," Jessie asked, still confused, "why did those people go away angry?"

"Because," Anne Wiley said, "this sly creature never had any intentions of selling Spy to them."

"Didn't you want your nephew to have him?" Jessie asked, more confused than ever. "Didn't you want to keep him in the family?"

"My dear girl," Mr. Yon said solemnly, "did you see the expression on my nephew's face? Did you see the downturned mouth, the unkind eyes? Do you think I would let my good friend"—he reached out to pat Northern Spy—"spend his life with someone like that? No. I was desperate to find a way to keep that from happening. A way that would not cause a family rift."

"And my riding made that possible?" Jessie asked, looking from one person to another for some kind of explanation.

"Not your riding, exactly," Kate said, and laughed again. "Mr. Yon told them that they were just minutes too late. That he had only this morning agreed to sell Spy to you!"

Looking embarrassed, Mr. Yon said, "A lie, I know. But sometimes ..." He let the rest of the sentence hang.

"So now that you've been so clever, what are you going to do with Spy?" Anne Wiley asked. "By my count, eight prospective buyers have been here to see Spy, and you haven't approved of any of them."

"Yes." Mr. Yon sighed mournfully. "That's true." He gazed helplessly at Anne.

"Oh, no," Anne said. "You're not going to pass that responsibility off on me!"

"No, no, of course not. I would never expect you to sell him," Mr. Yon said. "But if you could keep him for a little while ... just until I have time to think about this problem ... take him to eventing competitions, let him be seen, expose his talents to the riding public. Perhaps someone worthy of him will come along." Here he flicked a quick look at Kate. "Then you can simply refer that person to me. Is that too much to ask of an old friend?" he asked.

"*Who* would ride him?" Anne asked, rattling her crutches to emphasize her point. "*Who* would take him to shows?"

Mr. Yon looked hopefully at Kate.

"I have my hands full with Night Owl," Kate said. "But what about Jessie? Jessie can ride him! Can't she?"

Jessie looked eagerly from Kate to Mr. Yon. Was she just imagining things, or was there a flicker of disappointment in Mr. Yon's eyes?

"That is a possibility," he said slowly.

"A possibility! It's the perfect solution!" Kate said excitedly. "You saw how great she looked on him just now. Jessie, just think of it!" Happiness was bubbling through her words.

"Well?" Anne said, looking first at Jessie and then at Pietro. "What do you two think?"

"She thinks it's wonderful, he thinks it's wonderful," Kate said before either of them could

answer. "How could they think anything else?
We'll be able to event together, Jessie—the three
of us. You, me, and Dara. Wait, where *is* Dara?"
Kate stood on tiptoe to look around. "Wait until
she hears this. When can we have him?"

"Kate!" her mother said, and laughed. "Calm
down! Give Jessie and Pietro a chance to say
something."

Mr. Yon looked at Jessie. "Well, little one, what
do you say? You looked very good on Spy just
now. And your eyes"—he bent down to stare at
her solemnly—"are very kind."

"They are," Kate agreed instantly. "Jessie's the
kindest person in the world."

It seemed to Jessie that the whole world had
stopped moving to wait for her answer. There
wasn't a reason she could think of to say no.

"She's going to say yes," Kate said, leaning
forward a little to hear the word.

"Yes," Jessie said softly.

"Hurray!" Kate shouted, and turned to Mr. Yon.
"Now, when can we have him?"

Chapter 4

ONE afternoon two weeks later, Jessie hopped off the school bus. She was halfway up her driveway before she noticed that her grandmother's car was parked in it. Quickening her steps, she came in the back door of the low ranch house with a happy smile on her face. "Hi, Gran," she said, bending to kiss the slim, vibrant woman who was waiting for her.

"Hello there, snooks," her grandmother said in a voice that was surprisingly deep for such a little person. Mrs. Edwards was Jessie's mother's mother. In her working days she'd been a radio actress. "I got all the man-stealing parts because of my voice," she loved to tell people. "Then television came in. The body didn't match the voice, so I was out of work."

"What are you doing here?" Jessie asked, dropping her books and then pouring herself a glass of milk.

"That's not much of a welcome!" Gran said, and pretended to pout.

37

Jessie grinned. "You know I love seeing you, Gran. I just didn't expect it today."

"Mrs. McPhaden had to leave early again," Gran said. "So I'm filling in."

Jessie frowned. "That's the third time in two weeks!" she said.

Her grandmother shrugged. "She's got some problems that she can't seem to work out. You know her husband was in a car accident, and she's having trouble finding someone to take him to his physical therapy sessions. Unfortunately, her problems become your dad's problems when she can't be here."

"I hope she can straighten things out," Jessie said as she finished the milk and rinsed the glass. "I sure don't want to go through finding a new housekeeper, especially since Sarah and Nick like Mrs. Mac so much."

"I hope things get ironed out, too," Gran said, "because much as I love coming over here, I have more travel plans coming up. Well," she said, and sighed, "we'll just keep our fingers crossed. And now, while I've got you all to myself, I want to hear about the big news. I go away for a few weeks and all sorts of things happen!"

Puzzled, Jessie looked at her. "Oh, you mean Northern Spy," she said after a minute.

"What a grand name," Mrs. Edwards said. "It has such a handsome, daring ring to it."

"If that's the case, it fits him to a tee," Jessie said. "He's probably the most beautiful horse I've ever ridden."

"Tell me how it all happened," her grandmother said, settling down in her chair as if preparing to be completely enthralled.

Jessie told the story, embellishing it a little for her grandmother's benefit—making it funny and leaving out the parts about how nervous she'd been on Spy.

"Isn't he something, that Mr. Yon. I bet I'd like him. And aren't you lucky!" Gran said, and beamed. She reached over to touch Jessie's hand. "I'm so happy for you. It's about time you had a little good luck. You know, I worry about you a lot."

"You don't have to worry about me," Jessie said. "I'm fine."

"Are you?" Her grandmother's eyes examined her closely. "There are times lately when I'm not so sure of that."

"Of course I am," Jessie said firmly. "Well, I admit I may get a little moody now and then, but basically I'm okay." She fell silent for a minute, then looked at her grandmother. "I admit that for a while there it seemed as though everybody I knew was moving along while I was stuck in quicksand. But all that's changed now," she said, and beamed at her grandmother. "I've got a horse of my own—well, just about," she amended. "The way Mr. Yon is going about selling Spy, I'll be old and gray before he finds a buyer."

"And is that what pleases you so much? The fact that Spy is yours ... just about?" her grandmother asked curiously.

"Of course," Jessie said, surprised at the question. "I've wanted a horse of my own for ages. Didn't you know that?"

"No. I must say, that's one thing you've kept pretty much to yourself."

Jessie considered that for a minute. "Come to think of it, I probably have," she agreed.

Over the last few years, with her mother being so sick, there had never seemed to be a right time to talk about something as frivolous as wanting a horse. If Jessie had mentioned it to anyone, it had been to Time-Out or Kate—and Kate certainly wouldn't have mentioned it to Jessie's grandmother.

"And your friends, they have horses, too?" Gran asked.

"My best friends do. That's what makes having Spy so perfect. Kate and Dara are terrific riders. They're probably the best combined-training riders in the state. And one of these days they're going to end up riding in the Olympics."

"Oh, my," her grandmother said. Then she leaned forward and whispered, "What's combined training?"

Jessie laughed and explained about combined training—showing a horse in the dressage arena performing complex maneuvers in front of the judges, then on a cross-country course that was almost like a steeplechase, and finally, stadium jumping—all three disciplines part of the same event.

"Oh, my," her grandmother said again. "That *is* impressive. And you do that kind of riding, too?" Jessie nodded. "And do you want to end up in the Olympics someday, too?"

"Of course," Jessie said emphatically—but her eyes didn't quite meet her grandmother's. "That's what this hard work is all about." Isn't it? she asked herself.

"Well, I'm meeting a new Jessie Robeson today," said Gran. "I had no idea there was this competitive side to you. It's wonderful to have a dream," she went on. "When I was a young girl and I wanted to be an actress, I had to fight my parents tooth and nail for the chance. It was hard work, and some people would say I missed a lot of fun, but not me. The work was fun! I was doing what I wanted to be doing. Nothing feels better than that. Good for you, Jessie," Gran said, leaning over to give her a hug.

Then Mrs. Edwards sat back in her chair. "Well," she said. "I have a surprise of my own to tell you about. But I wonder, after what you've just told me, if my timing might be poor."

"What is it?" Jessie asked. In the old days, when Jessie's mother had still been alive, Gran had been full of surprises. But over the last few years no one in the family had felt much like being surprised about anything.

"Well, I'm going to spill the beans to the rest of the family at dinner, but I'll let you in on it now. I told you that I was upset because I thought you were still quite depressed. And I know that your dad is only getting things back together in his own life. So I thought, what always peps me up when I'm low? And the answer is—a trip!"

She waited for a second, but Jessie just stared at her.

"A trip, snooks," repeated her grandmother. "To someplace new and exciting." She snapped her fingers in the air over her head. "Spain, maybe? Or *bella Italia*?"

"Europe?" Jessie said.

"Of course! When I say a trip, I mean a trip! Well, what do you think?"

"I think that's very generous," Jessie said slowly.

"Generous. Hmmm," her grandmother said. " 'Generous' is not quite the word I was looking for. I was looking more for—say—fantastic! Stupendous! Even oh, boy!"

"Oh, Gran, I'm sorry," Jessie said. "It *is* fantastic and stupendous—and *expensive*. You don't have to do this for us!"

"I know it's expensive," Gran answered calmly. "But your mother was my only daughter. Everything I have will someday belong to you children. I didn't get a chance to see my daughter enjoy any of it, and I'm not going to make the same mistake with you kids. So hang the expense! Full steam ahead!"

"Oh boy," Jessie said. Her grandmother laughed and hugged her.

"Gran, this is all so unbelievable—but I can't stay and talk anymore. I've got to get to the barn. Will you be here for supper?"

"Duty calls, does it?" said her grandmother. "Well, I understand devotion. And yes, I'll be here for dinner. We'll talk more about the trip then. I'd better get busy myself, anyway. I have a rather complicated recipe here."

"You're not roasting some lamb?" Jessie asked. Her grandmother was many wonderful things, but a cook wasn't one of them. She had one stock company dinner, roast leg of lamb with garlic. Jessie hated it, but she'd never had the heart to confess that fact to her grandmother.

"No, love, not tonight," her grandmother said sorrowfully. "By the time I got over here, Mrs. Mac had all the ingredients for something called—uh, enchiladas? Have you ever had them?"

"No," Jessie said. It wasn't exactly the truth. She'd had them, but not the way her grandmother would cook them—she'd bet her life on it.

"Well, they look complicated. But we'll see." Suddenly her tone changed. "Jessie," she said, picking up the recipe card and pretending to study it, "you don't want to go to Europe, do you?"

Jessie felt terrible. What her grandmother said was true—she didn't want to go. But she hadn't realized it showed until now. "Gran, what are you talking about?" she said, choosing her words carefully. "Who wouldn't want to go to Europe? It's just that the news took me so much by surprise!"

Her grandmother studied her closely, and Jessie kept a happy smile on her face. "How do you think Sarah and Nick will take to the idea?" asked Gran.

"If you could find a tour that included some Little League fields, you'd have a better chance with Nick. If Sarah can take her Pooh Bear, she'll go anywhere."

"It'll be fun," her grandmother said, "and good for all of you."

"Of course it will," Jessie agreed. But in her heart she wasn't so sure.

Chapter 5

By the time Jessie got to Windcroft, Kate and Dara had finished their warm-up in the ring and were starting to jump. Jessie saddled Spy hurriedly —which was a mistake. She had already discovered that Spy picked up any tension she was feeling. And most of the time he was already tense enough on his own. Jessie forced herself to slow down and headed him up the path.

"Zowie," Kate said when Jessie caught up to them. There was a touch of awe in her voice. "Look at him go."

"What's he doing?" Jessie said anxiously as she rode Spy into the practice ring. His normal stride had been extended by at least a foot.

"I've never seen a horse extend like that, so easily," Dara said. "What did you do?"

"I'm not sure," Jessie said, reining Spy to a halt. "He's uptight because I rushed him through his grooming. Then I think I gave him a little more leg than I wanted to, and to make up for it I

44

pulled back a little on the reins—and you saw what happened."

"It was beautiful," Kate said. "See if you can do it again."

"Again?" Jessie asked nervously. In the past two weeks these surprises on Spy had become a little too regular for Jessie to be completely happy about them. Every once in a while she gave him what she thought was her usual signal, and his response caught her off guard. She had almost decided that he knew more about this riding business than she did.

Now she urged Spy into a slow trot alongside the rail. At the corner she turned him on a diagonal line across the ring, squeezed her legs, and pulled back slightly on the reins.

Spy took off again.

Kate and Dara laughed delightedly. "If I didn't know better," Dara said, "I'd think you two had been working together for years. I wonder what else he knows that we don't know he knows."

"You're ready to event him, you know," Kate said authoritatively.

"Oh no, I'm not," Jessie answered, shaking her head emphatically. "It may look great to you, but most of what's happening between me and Spy is totally accidental."

"Don't be ridiculous," Kate said. "You've got the novice class in your back pocket. I really think you should ride him Saturday at Spruce Ridge. It's just a local horse trial—no big deal. It's a good place to get into eventing competition again. You've been out of it for almost a year. No wonder you're nervous!"

Jessie glanced at Dara. "What do you think?" she asked.

Dara shrugged. "Kate may be right. It's always nerve-wracking to show if you haven't done it for a while. I think Spy's ready for the novice class, at least."

"Besides," Kate urged, "it was part of your agreement with Mr. Yon, remember? He said you should compete on Spy so that people will get to see him." She turned to Dara. "Can you imagine the kind of splash Jessie's going to make on Spy? Anytime anybody brings a new horse to an event people get excited, even if he's only an old plug. But Spy! Wow!"

"I agree, Jessie. His jumping's great, his dressage work is great. He sometimes gets a little strong on the trails, but that's no big deal. Enter him!" Dara said.

Jessie sighed. She wanted to remind Kate that Kate had been the one making agreements with Mr. Yon, not Jessie. But maybe Kate and Dara were right. Maybe this nagging, uncomfortable feeling she had whenever she rode Spy was just nerves from not having ridden him regularly.

After all, he hadn't done anything to make Jessie think she couldn't control him. His problem—if you could call it a problem—was not that he didn't do what she asked, but that he did what she asked so much more thoroughly than she felt equipped to handle.

Jessie looked at her friends' expectant faces. She couldn't think of any excuse that they'd accept. And no matter who had done the negotiating, showing Spy *had* been part of the agreement with Mr. Yon.

"Okay," she said. "I'll do it."

"Terrific!" Kate said happily. Then her smile

faded. "I don't know why I'm so happy to have you compete," she said in mock depression. "If Spy gets any better, you'll be beating me and the Owl."

"That'll be the day," Jessie said.

"Okay, team! Now that it's all settled, let's try the jumps again," Dara said.

"Let me do the first rounds," Jessie said. "I have to get home early tonight. Mrs. Mac had to leave again, and my grandmother's staying for supper."

"Lord have mercy," Kate said, "roast leg of lamb again!"

"No," Jessie said, and laughed, "enchiladas."

"You were lucky this time," Kate said. "One of these days you're going to have to tell your grandmother how you really feel about lamb."

Jessie circled Spy, making sure he'd seen and accepted all the jumps. She didn't want any unpleasant surprises, like Spy's deciding in midstride that he needed a better look at the rail fence she was asking him to go over. Jessie wanted to be especially sure Spy knew what he was in for.

"Take your time," Dara said. "Don't rush him. Give yourself a minute to scope out the best line before you actually start."

Don't rush him! Jessie said to herself. That was a laugh! Obviously neither Dara nor Kate realized how little Jessie had to do with when and how Spy jumped.

Jessie looked at the gate, trying to determine the best approach, the one that would minimize the difficulties of the oxer that came right behind it. If she and Spy negotiated the oxer correctly, the brush jump and the rails would fall easily into place. Well, she had her version of how this jumping round should go. Now it was time to see what Spy thought.

Jessie brought Spy to a controlled canter and approached the gate. She could tell Spy realized he was going to be asked to jump. His ears flicked forward, and she could feel the electricity in his body.

Control! Jessie thought. She tried to force Spy to maintain an even pace through the pressure of her legs and the weight of her seat in the saddle, but Spy hadn't reached what Jessie considered the logical takeoff point when she felt him start to rise.

Jessie wasn't prepared, but she managed to come forward herself—bending at her hips, crouching near Spy's neck, keeping herself over his center of gravity. Her hands went forward to follow the pull of his head, giving him all the freedom he needed to negotiate the jump.

Now he was over. Jessie felt the shock of his landing through her whole body. She absorbed it as best she could through her knees and ankles— and almost before she had regained her balance, the oxer was looming in front of them.

She was better prepared this time because she knew that Spy was also going to take this jump earlier than she had planned. The oxer went beautifully.

Spy had so much power! Jessie could feel it bunching under her like an explosion ready to happen. But he didn't explode—he completed the jumps and came to a halt nicely when Jessie asked him to. It wasn't until he had stopped completely that Jessie realized how nervous she had been.

She turned to look at Kate and Dara, sure they could tell she'd been in trouble. But they were both smiling delightedly. "That was beautiful!" Dara said. "He's a natural. Do you want to go again?"

"No," Jessie said quickly. "You go ahead. I'll walk him a bit."

They each jumped three rounds, and by the end of the third one, Jessie and Spy had reached a kind of truce. She might not be the one giving directions, but at least she was able to anticipate what Spy was going to do.

"Want to try them backward?" Kate asked.

"Not me," Jessie said. "I think I'm going to quit while things are going well. Besides, as I said, my grandmother's at the house."

"One of these days you have to meet Jessie's grandmother," Kate told Dara. "You'll love her."

"She's got this big surprise she wants to spring on Dad and the kids," said Jessie.

"What?" Kate asked, reining Night Owl in and turning him to face Jessie.

"She wants to send us on a trip to Europe," Jessie said.

"Wow!" Kate gave a long whistle.

"You'll love it," Dara said.

"You've been to Europe already?" Kate asked Dara in mock annoyance. "I should have known." She turned to Jessie. "When? For how long?"

"We didn't get that far," Jessie said, heading Spy toward the gate. "But probably not all that long." She knew that Kate was thinking about riding, and competitions she was liable to miss. It was what was on her own mind, too.

Jessie walked Spy until she was sure he was cool, untacked him, and turned him out into a paddock. Then she went down the dark row of stalls to say hello to Time-Out.

The mare raised her head and stared at Jessie contemplatively.

"Don't I get a hello anymore?" Jessie asked.

At the sound of her voice, Time-Out moved to the stall door until she was close enough for Jessie to stroke her nose. In the back of the stall the colt lay stretched out on the soft bedding, fast asleep.

"You look down in the dumps," Jessie told the horse. "I'll bet I know why. Everybody's coming to say what a beautiful baby you've got, and you feel forgotten." Time-Out nickered softly. "Well, I haven't forgotten you. I'll love you as long as I live," Jessie told her.

"And if you happen to hear that I've got this new horse to ride, don't worry. It won't change a thing. Even if you happen to hear how gorgeous he is, which he is, and that I'm going to event him, which I am, the whole thing was Kate's doing. If it had been up to me, I'd still be mooning around, waiting for you. I'd give almost anything if it *was* you I was going to ride," she added. "This Spy is a handful, and a big responsibility. Kate and Dara say I look great on him and that we're sure to win a ribbon—but you know that was never important to me. Which is a good thing, I guess. Remember all the mistakes we made in the beginning? But then we got our act together, didn't we, girl?"

Quietly Jessie opened the stall door and went inside. Time-Out nuzzled her shoulder, and Jessie laid her head down on the mare's warm brown withers.

She wondered if Time-Out had any idea that her days at Windcroft were numbered. She wondered if Mrs. Jesper would be as careful about Time-Out's new owner as Mr. Yon had been about Spy's. Somehow she doubted it.

"Sometimes life isn't very fair," she told the mare despondently.

Time-Out turned her solemn eyes on Jessie and blinked as if she understood completely. Jessie blinked back, trying to keep her own eyes from overflowing. "Oh, one more thing. My grandmother wants to send us all to Europe." Time-Out moved restlessly and snorted. "I think it's kind of silly myself. Can you imagine Nick and Sarah in Italy? Well"—Jessie gave Time-Out one last pat—"I'll see you tomorrow ... that is, if Mrs. Mac doesn't have to leave early and I end up babysitting for the kids."

"What's this stuff?" Nick asked an hour later, tentatively pushing a fork into the sauce-covered mass on his plate.

"Enchiladas, snooks," Gran said as she put the basket of bread on the table and sat down herself.

Nick wrinkled his nose and looked at his father. "When's Mrs. Mac coming back?" he asked.

"Soon, I hope," Mr. Robeson said. "These look wonderful," he said, sounding a bit uncertain. He smiled at Mrs. Edwards.

"Well then, eat up." She was beaming.

Jessie bravely took a forkful, placed it in her mouth, chewed—and then relaxed. She looked over at Nick, who was eyeing her intently. It's okay, she told him silently. Try some. Still looking doubtful, Nick tasted the enchilada.

"Hey!" he said in surprise. "These look a little weird, but they're good!" Gran looked delighted.

"I have something exciting to tell all of you," Jessie said. Everyone turned to her. "I'm going to be riding Spy in an event on Saturday."

"Already?" her father said.

"Kate and Dara say I'm ready," Jessie said, trying to sound convinced herself.

"I've never been to a horse show," Gran said. "Saturday, you say? I wonder if I can make it."

"Oh, don't bother," Jessie said quickly. "It's not an important show, just a schooling event."

"That wouldn't bother me," Gran said. "After hearing all about your new horse, I'm rather anxious to see him. Maybe we should all go?" She glanced around the table.

"Sounds good to me," Mr. Robeson said.

"Me, too," Sarah called out excitedly.

"I have a baseball game," Nick reminded his dad.

"Oh, that's right," Mr. Robeson said, looking unhappily at Jessie.

"Don't worry about it, Dad. Go to the game with Nick," said Jessie. "To be honest with you, I'm not ready to have you all come and watch. I think you should wait until later in the season, when Spy and I are more of a team."

"Really?" her grandmother asked.

"Really," Jessie insisted. The last thing she wanted was the pressure of her family there watching. It would make her even more nervous than she already was.

"Well, all right," Mrs. Edwards said. "We'll wait a bit, until you tell us you're ready. Now I have something exciting to talk to you about. Jessie already knows what it is. I want you all to close your eyes and think about the most beautiful place in the world—the place where you would most like to spend some time."

"Why?" Sarah asked.

"Never mind, snooks, just do it." Jessie watched while her brother and sister squinched their eyes closed tight. "You, too, Gordon," Mrs. Edwards said to Jessie's father. "Are you all thinking?" They nodded.

"Good. Now here's my surprise. Wherever you're thinking of, you can actually go there! I want to give the four of you a vacation to end all vacations."

"Really?" Nick's eyes flew open with excitement. "Granny, thanks. Thanks a hundred billion times!" he said, jumping up from the table and running to give his grandmother a big hug.

"Now, *that's* the kind of reaction I was looking for," Mrs. Edwards said. "You must want to go to a very special place, Nick. Tell us where it is."

"Shea Stadium," Nick said proudly. "The Mets are my absolute favorite team."

"But that's in New York!" Gran said. "One state away from here!"

"I know it's far," Nick said, "but you said anywhere we wanted to go. You promised!"

"Well, I know but—" Gran looked helplessly at her son-in-law.

"And I want to go to the Bronx Zoo," Sarah said loudly. "That's far away, too."

Jessie looked from her brother and sister to her father to her grandmother. There was a moment of strained silence, and then the adults burst out laughing.

Mr. Robeson leaned over and took Gran's hand.

"If it's any consolation, I was thinking about Switzerland."

"Well, that's more what I had in mind, Gordon," Gran said.

"It was a nice thought, but I guess this family isn't quite ready for that kind of trip."

"I only wanted to give you all a little happiness," Gran said wistfully.

"And you will. We'll take Nick to Shea, and Sarah to the zoo, and"—he turned to look at Jessie—"where do you want to go, honey?"

"No place," Jessie said.

"No place?" her father echoed. "Come on now. You have to come up with something."

"If she can't, can I have her turn?" Nick asked.

"No, you cannot," his father said.

"I can't come up with anything right now. Let me think about it for a while," Jessie said.

"Well! I'm certainly going to end up getting off cheap on this one!" Gran said. "I'll just put the money I was going to spend on the trip aside until you can come up with a way to spend it."

"What do we say to Grandma?" Mr. Robeson asked.

"Thank you," Nick and Sarah sang.

"For everything," Jessie added softly.

Chapter 6

THE week before the horse trial passed quickly—too quickly. Jessie decided there must be a law of nature that said that the more you didn't want time to pass, the faster it went.

Now it was the night before the event, and the three girls were in the barn preparing their horses for competition. The animals had been thoroughly brushed and had had their hooves cleaned and polished. Their tails had been shampooed and now they were having their manes braided.

Braiding was time-consuming and sometimes nerve-racking, especially with a horse like Spy who thought standing still was a punishment. But it changed the horses into glorious-looking animals. The tiny knots of mane, secured with bright bits of wool, outlined the curves of the horses' necks and made them seem even stronger and more muscular than they were. Before the manes were braided, horses were beautiful. Afterward, they were suddenly elegant as well—and a little mysterious-looking. Once it was finished, braiding always seemed worthwhile.

Jessie always thought that the same thing happened to the girls when they dressed in their riding clothes. When they pulled their hair back into formal knots or braids and tucked it up under their velvet riding hats; when they slipped on their riding jackets, jodhpurs, crisp white shirts, and stocks; when they kicked off their sneakers and put on the high boots, polished to look like black satin—then good old Kate and Dara and Jessie disappeared. In their places stood three refined, sophisticated young ladies.

It was easier to make the change in themselves, since they were more willing than the horses. Jessie did the last braid on Spy—running a strand of royal blue wool through the hair, doubling the braid back on itself, and securing it at the base of Spy's neck with a double twist of yarn.

Then she stepped back to look at him, rolling her shoulders to get rid of the ache in her back muscles, and fighting down the thought that all this fussing had taken more out of her than she cared to give. With Time-Out, she'd never doubted that it had been necessary. Jessie felt that she was doing something to give the mare an added edge. But Spy needed an added edge the way a razor blade did.

Jessie looked down the aisle to see how Dara and Kate were doing, and compared Northern Spy with Arpeggio and Night Owl in the process. She was certainly no expert—but it wouldn't take an expert to see that of the three animals, Northern Spy was the most beautiful.

His conformation was perfect. At least Jessie

could find no fault with it. He had a fine head, with large bright eyes and an alert expression. "What's next?" his eyes always seemed to be asking. His back was strong and just long enough to be right, with the ribs wide behind the girth. His hindquarters were rounded, blending into strong muscular thighs, and all of it was contained in a coat of satinlike chestnut.

Besides all the obvious physical perfection, there was some magic about Spy you couldn't put your finger on. All you could tell when you looked at him was that he was an extraordinary horse. When he was duded up in his braids and polished tack, he would be hard to equal.

And riding this fantastic example of horseflesh would be—*ta da*—Jessica Claire Robeson. The idea seemed so ridiculous to Jessie that she had to put it out of her mind. If she allowed herself to dwell on it, she'd end up not going through with the event.

"Finished?" Kate asked, looking up to find Jessie watching her.

"Yup. They don't call me Nimble Fingers for nothing. Want some help?" she asked Kate.

"I'm done, too. So what's left?"

"Nothing that I can think of," Jessie said, gathering up her leftover wool and heading for the tack room to put it away.

"I just have to put some clean wood chips in Arpeggio's stall before I put him back," Dara said as she followed Jessie to the tack room with her ball of dark green wool. "Don't they all look magnificent?" she asked Jessie.

"They should," Jessie said. "They've just been through the equivalent of a weekend at Elizabeth Arden's."

"I knew a kid at Concordia who bleached her horse's mane and tail." Concordia was the stable in Pennsylvania where Dara had kept Arpeggio before the family moved to Smithfield.

"Get out," Jessie said, staring at Dara. "What'd she do that for?"

"She thought it made him stand out more. He was a nondescript brown."

"How'd he look?" Jessie asked, fascinated.

"Outstanding," Dara said. "Ridiculous, but certainly outstanding."

"What time is it?" Kate called.

Still laughing at Dara's story, Jessie checked the clock in the tack room. "Almost eight," she said, walking back into the aisle to watch Kate finish grooming Night Owl.

"I'd better get a move on," Kate said.

"Must be time for the daily call from Pete Hastings," Dara commented. "Have you asked him out yet?"

"No," Kate said. "I haven't had a free weekend yet. Have you asked Doug?"

"There's no event next weekend," Dara said, without answering Kate's questions.

"I know. Maybe I'll sort of nudge him into a date for next Saturday night. One good thing about this long-term telephone friendship—by the time I do get to go out with him I won't be nervous."

"Well, I'm nervous," Dara said.

There was a pause. Kate looked at Jessie. "It can't be the event giving her nerves," she said. Jessie nodded her head in agreement. "What do you think it is?" Kate asked.

"Don't know," Jessie said. "Let's ask her."

The girls turned to Dara and asked in unison, "Why?"

Dara grinned. "Well ..." She dragged the word out as she continued shoveling the used bedding from Arpeggio's stall into a wheelbarrow.

"Well, what?" Kate asked impatiently.

"Well, as it turns out, I don't have to ask Doug out. He drove me home from school today and asked me to go to the movies with him tomorrow night."

"After the event?" Jessie said in surprise.

"Well, I told him I probably wouldn't get back until pretty late, so we're aiming for the late movie. If we don't make that, we'll just go out for a hamburger or something."

"You made a date with Doug Lyons for the night of a horse trial?" Jessie repeated in amazement. "Isn't the tension of competing enough for you? If I did that, the pressure would blow the top of my head off!"

Kate turned to Jessie, her eyes wide. "But, Jessica, we're talking to Dara 'the Cool' Cooper," she said, "not to an ordinary mortal like you or me."

"Oh, that's right. Sorry," Jessie said, still staring at Dara. "For a minute there I forgot."

"I'm not all that cool," Dara said. She dumped the last of the bedding into the wheelbarrow, leaned on the pitchfork, and looked at her friends. "I figured this trial wasn't that big a deal. It's only a schooling event, and I've already turned Doug down twice."

"Twice?" Kate squealed. "Did you know about this, Jessie?"

"Oh, stop. It wasn't anything," Dara said, and giggled. "You know—kind of, want to stop for a soda on the way home from school? And I had to say no because of riding and all. So I decided that this time I'd say yes."

"Simple," Jessie said to Kate.

"Nothing to it," Kate agreed. "She's going out with the best-looking boy in the entire school on the same day that she's eventing, but what's the big deal?"

"I told you I was nervous," Dara said.

"Nervous does not begin to describe how you should be feeling," Kate said.

"No way. You should be frothing at the mouth, and your knees should be shaking," Jessie told her sternly.

"Oh!" Dara exclaimed as if a light had suddenly gone on in her head. "I didn't realize that. How's this?" she asked. She pushed the wheelbarrow out of the barn, her knees flapping together with every step.

Grinning, Kate snipped the last end of yarn from Night Owl's braids.

"Well, Big Bird," she said to the horse who had been her constant friend for the last four years, "you are totally gorgeous. I can't wait for tomorrow, can you? I'm happy you guys are spending the night so we can all be excited together," she added, turning to Jessie. "Let's put them in and head for the showers. If Pete calls while I'm washing up, you can talk to him. Maybe you can jog him into action."

"Thanks," Jessie said with a touch of sarcasm. "Always ready to help a friend."

Dara, who had taken her shower last, toweled her hair dry and said, "So which room has the ghost?"

"The den," Kate said from her bed where she was sitting cross-legged, polishing her nails. "At least that's where Popsie used to have fits." Popsie had been Kate's collie. She had lived a long, full life at the farm and had died last year. "She'd get all cowardly in there—whine and carry on with her tail between her legs." Slowly Kate drew a brushful of Pink Parfait enamel over the thumbnail on her left hand.

"Have you ever seen it?" Dara asked, running a comb through her short, blond hair until it lay like a neat cap around her head.

Kate handed Jessie the nail polish and held out her right hand so Jessie could paint those nails. "Nope. Popsie's the only one, and we never could get her to talk about it."

"I thought you were getting a new dog," Jessie said, carefully drawing the brush down Kate's nail.

"We are, soon as Mom's off her crutches. You're doing a great job, by the way. Want me to polish yours?" Kate asked, watching gratefully as Jessie worked. "I just can't get my left hand to be neat about putting polish on my right hand."

"No, thanks," Jessie said. "I can't be bothered touching them up."

"Let's go down and sit in the den and see if it shows up!" Dara suggested excitedly.

"Let's not, you mean," Jessie said.

"Come on," Dara urged, walking toward the doorway. "Just for an hour. It's still too early to go to bed."

"It'll be a waste of time," Kate said unwinding her long legs and standing up. "I've tried before. We won't see it."

Dara just ignored her. "Bring that candle," she ordered, pointing to the candlestick that stood on

Kate's dresser because the power went out so often in the country.

"If you're going to sit there in the dark, I'd just as soon wait here," Jessie said.

"Not in the dark." Dara reached for Jessie's hand, and pulled her out of the room. "We'll light the candle!"

But when they were settled in the dimly lit room, with the candle casting big, flickering shadows on the walls, Jessie thought that the dark might have been better.

"Isn't this eerie?" Dara said happily. "How old is this place, anyway?"

"Most of it was built in the early 1800s," Kate said.

"That's so neat! I'd love to live in an old house."

"It is nice," Kate agreed. "I've never seen a ghost, but I do have a feeling of company from all the lives that have been lived here."

Jessie felt that way, too. Maybe that was why she loved coming here. There'd been an emptiness in her own house since her mom's death. It was getting better. Now that Mrs. Mac was with them, the house had almost become a home again. But if Mrs. Mac had to be replaced, who knew how things would be after that?

"I think the gold sweater. What do you think?" Kate was staring at Jessie. "To wear when she goes out with Doug," she explained patiently when Jessie didn't answer. "I think Dara should wear that big gold Shaker sweater, don't you?"

Jessie just stared at Kate. If the Robesons' home life was about to fall apart again, did it really matter what Dara wore on her date? Besides, whatever she ended up wearing would be right because Dara would be wearing it.

"Jessie? Are you okay?" Kate asked.

No, Jessie wanted to say. I'm not. I feel as though I've been boxed into a corner. I feel as if I don't have any control over the things that are happening in my life.

But she forced those feelings back down. It was no use talking about them. "Jessie is gone," she said in a deep, hollow voice. "I am the ghost of Christmas past."

Dara stared at her in amazement. Kate, catching Jessie's eye and winking, reached out and unobtrusively snuffed the candle, plunging the room into darkness. Dara gave a piercing shriek.

"Kate! Is something wrong?" Marc Wiley, Kate's dad, called from the other room.

"We're being haunted!" Kate called back.

"Really?" Anne Wiley's voice was excited. In a second the girls heard the hurried thump-thump of her crutches on the hall floor.

Kate reached out and turned on the table lamp. "Don't bother, Mom, we were just teasing Dara."

"Very funny," Dara said. She slouched down in her chair, a disgusted look on her face.

"Nuts," Mrs. Wiley said dejectedly from the doorway. "I really want to meet that ghost. Maybe we should leave him some cookies?"

"That's for Santa Claus, Mrs. Wiley," Jessie said, and grinned.

"Well, it worked for him," Anne Wiley said. "Don't you remember how every Christmas morning the cookies would be gone?"

"Don't *you* remember how every Christmas morning we used to find crumbs on Popsie's mouth?" Kate rejoined.

"Okay," Mrs. Wiley said, and laughed. "If you're not going to leave the poor ghost a snack, I think you three should toddle off to bed. It's after ten."

"It is?" Kate asked in surprise, and glanced quickly at the telephone.

A mean little spark of pleasure flickered in Jessie. Pete hadn't called. Somebody else's life wasn't running perfectly either. Then she closed her eyes, ashamed of herself. What kind of friend was she to be happy at that thought? After all Kate had done for her, too!

"Is she communicating with the ghost of Christmas yet to come?" Jessie opened her eyes to find Dara staring at her.

"Nope," Jessie said decisively, standing up. "No more ghosts tonight." Not the kind that Dara had been waiting for, nor the kind that had been plaguing Jessie for the last hour. "I'm going to bed."

"I guess we all might as well," Dara said, and yawned.

They were halfway up the stairs when the telephone rang.

"Kate," Mr. Wiley called, "it's for you."

"That's Pete!" Kate squealed, her face lighting up. Turning around, she hurried back downstairs.

"Fifteen minutes," her father said sternly as he handed Kate the telephone.

I'm *glad* he called, I'm *glad*, Jessie told herself, and was relieved to find it was true.

Chapter 7

THE splash that Northern Spy made at the horse trial was even bigger than Kate had predicted. Jessie could hardly turn around without someone asking her where the horse had come from. Dara and Kate grinned gleefully whenever anyone said anything. Jessie could tell that they were happy for her, pleased with the attention she was getting.

She wished she could share in their feelings, but attention wasn't something she looked forward to when she was in the ring—at least not the kind of attention she was getting now. Jessie felt as if people expected her to live up to Spy, and she wasn't sure she could do it. She wasn't even sure she *wanted* to do it.

She got through the dressage test by concentrating with every brain cell she had so that she wouldn't do something dumb and make Spy look bad. Judging from the way people were watching the gelding now, Mr. Yon would probably get a million calls tonight from people who wanted to buy him—as long as Jessie could keep him looking good.

She was only doing the novice dressage test, using the same skills she'd practiced with Time-Out—but Spy pushed the limits of every move. He kept wanting to do a little more, go a little faster, step a little higher, so that Jessie had to control him every inch of the way. By the time they had completed the test and she had bowed to the judge, the white shirt she wore under her dark blue riding jacket was drenched with sweat.

Dara and Kate were waiting for her, their faces ecstatic under their black velvet riding hats. "You were wonderful!" Kate gasped. "That was amazing!"

Jessie was still too keyed up to smile back. "Hold him while I dismount," she said, handing Kate the reins. When her feet touched the ground, her legs almost buckled. She had to grab on to the saddle for balance.

"What's the matter?" Dara asked quickly.

"Nothing," Jessie said, "I missed my step, that's all."

"I wish we had a video camera," Kate went on. "If only you could have seen yourself. That was the most beautiful novice test I've ever seen. You had him completely under control, yet you could sense how much power there was in him, just waiting to—"

"Explode," Jessie said.

"Right!" Kate said, smiling delightedly. "It was wonderful. You've won the class, no question about it."

"I think Kate's right," Dara added. "I know you're a good rider, but you were even better than I thought. You handled him beautifully every step of the way."

"Thanks," Jessie said. What Dara said was true. She *had* handled Spy every step of the way, so she deserved some of the credit for his performance. And now she would have to handle him every step of the way on the outside course and then in the jumping ring. She just hoped she had enough stamina to do it.

Jessie found a shady spot to stand with Spy. She put a halter on him so he could crop the meager blades of grass around them without getting the bit in his bridle all messy. Then she waited for Dara and Kate to compete. She could see them from where she stood. Dara's test seemed very good to her, and so did Kate's, though Jessie thought Night Owl looked a little stiff compared to Arpeggio.

With the dressage portion of the competition over, the girls walked back to where the Windcroft Stables van was parked, untacked the horses, and put them in their stalls. Kate's dad, Marc Wiley, was sitting in a lawn chair nearby, talking to some other parents. Jessie heard Mr. Yon's name mentioned and assumed he was telling them Northern Spy's history.

At events, Mr. Wiley was the official chauffeur, as well as babysitter for the horses. Kate's mother was the official encourager and coach—when the girls needed it. But today she'd stayed at home.

Dara's mom only came to the bigger competitions. This one she considered little more than a practice session. "No big trainers for her to impress," was Dara's way of putting it. Mrs. Cooper was what Jessie and Kate referred to as a horse-show snob, and Dara would have been the first to agree with that assessment.

At first the frequent arguments between Dara and her mother had upset Jessie. But gradually she'd come to realize that they weren't mad at each other—they just saw things differently. After each of them had had her say, the air was cleared, and Dara and her mother went back to being friends. It was a puzzle to Jessie how people could disagree so completely and still love one another.

"We're going to get something to drink," Kate called to her father, "and then it's time for all the competitors to walk the cross-country course. Do you want a soda?"

Mr. Wiley waved a no-thank-you. The girls headed first to the refreshment stand and then to a hillside behind the dressage ring. From the top of the hill they could see most of the outside course. "That doesn't look too bad," Dara said.

Unlike the ring, where the jumps were odd-looking and sometimes garish, the jumps on the outside course were designed to look like natural obstacles a horse might encounter if he was riding along a trail. From where she stood, Jessie could pick out a pile of logs, then an immense tree trunk lying on the ground. Beyond that were a stone wall and a mock hayrack. Interspersed with these jumps were rails, gates, and hedges.

The girls found the first jump and approached it on the same line they would use when mounted. "This one's pretty straightforward," Dara said, gesturing at the pile of logs. They walked in a straight line to the next jump, a simple gate, and then to the tree trunk and then the stone wall.

"This one's tricky," Kate said. "If you come at it straight on, you're going to have to make a tight turn to stay on course for the rail over there." She pointed with her soda can.

"Right," Dara said.

Kate turned to look behind her. "So after you clear the tree trunk, you want to make a wide arc and come into the stone wall at an angle. That makes the approach to the rail a straighter line."

"Right," Dara said again. "Got that, Jessie?"

Jessie nodded.

They went over every jump that way, studying the line of approach until Kate was sure they had determined the best angle to jump it. When they had finished, Jessie's mind was reeling. She tried to calm herself. It seemed like a lot to remember— and it was. But her experience with Time-Out had been that once they started the course, the decisions Jessie had made on the walk-through turned out to be almost common sense, and she had no trouble remembering them. She hoped the same thing would happen today.

When they had determined the line for the last jump and had left the course, Kate said, "I'm starving. We have an hour before the event starts— let's get some lunch before we change into our cross-country clothes."

"I thought you'd never suggest it," Dara said. "You take more time with this stuff than my coaches did!"

"Walking the course is almost more important than jumping it," Kate told her.

"Yes, ma'am," Dara said giving her a mock salute, "but now *let's eat!*"

*   *   *

Jessie circled Spy, then sent him down the long approach to the practice jump set up inside the jumping ring. He jumped it cleanly, and she brought him to a complete halt after the landing. Stopping him like that was a way of getting his attention— telling him that just because he'd cleared the jump did not mean he had permission to take off at a dead run for the next obstacle. That was an idea he seemed to get every now and then.

On the outside course, a boy on an ungainly black mare was making his way stolidly over the jumps. The mare had no class and neither did the rider, but they managed to clear each jump in turn and crossed the finish line. The loudspeaker announced that the boy had incurred some time faults. That meant it had taken the team longer than the optimum time allotted to complete the course.

Neither the horse nor the rider seemed upset by that news. They just trotted blithely away. It was obvious that they were out to impress no one. "They're lucky," Jessie muttered as she gathered Spy up and turned him toward the starting box. One more horse, and it would be their turn on the outside course.

People were watching Jessie and whispering. At least she thought they were. Maybe she was paranoid. They weren't whispering about her, she was sure, but about Spy. Wondering, maybe, if he was as good as he looked, if his ability lived up to his beauty. Well, they were in for a surprise.

Jessie knew from practicing with Spy that he went over jumps the way he went around corners. Like quicksilver—his jumps were smooth, effortless, and strong. If he had one fault, it was his strength. It was going to be even harder containing him now than it had been during the dressage tests.

Jessie stared at the corners, wishing it was her turn already. This standing around thinking wasn't good for her nerves.

Now the palomino ahead of her had started— and he was in trouble. He stumbled in front of the stone wall, then jumped it poorly, and his rider was unable to bring him into the next jump on a good line. The next jump was the rail Kate had warned them about, and Jessie got a firsthand lesson in what would happen if she didn't keep her wits about her. The palomino came into the rails at an improbable angle, and—using more sense than his rider—refused to jump. The girl on his back lost her seat and fell, still holding on to the reins. She remounted and brought him back to the jump in a straight line. He went over it, but the refusal and fall had cost them in penalties.

It was Jessie's turn. She wiped her damp palms on her jodhpurs and put her leg to Spy.

He responded instantly, the way he always did. Jessie walked him into the starting box and waited for the signal to go. She hoped to hear it over the pounding of her heart.

The starter held a stopwatch in his hand. He began counting out loud, "Five, four, three, two, one ..."

Jessie's head was getting light, and her stomach was beginning to churn. If I faint, I won't have to do this, she told herself. Then the starter shouted "Go!"

At the word, she felt Spy gather himself to plunge forward. Instantly she restrained him, forcing him into a trot, then gradually allowing him to gather speed until he was cantering with long strides at a cross-country pace.

Jessie forced everything out of her mind except what she needed to know; she focused on the jump coming up and the feel of Spy under her. There were constant distractions on the course she hadn't counted on—judges standing at each jump, spectators clustered half-hidden at exciting portions of the course. Jessie tried to ignore them. She only hoped Spy would do the same thing.

But she needn't have worried. Spy was interested in one thing—the jumps.

The pile of logs was coming up now, and Spy was intrigued. His ears were forward, his whole attitude intent. He jumped it easily, looking at it curiously as he passed over it, then landed lightly. Jessie maintained an even pressure on him with her leg, holding him steady toward the second jump. He took this one, the gate, quickly—so quickly that Jessie almost got left behind. She regained her balance just in time to realize that if she didn't slow him down he was going to run right over the vertical tree trunk. She gave him several brief, sharp checks with the reins. That got enough of his attention so that he cleared the tree without mishap.

They were halfway to the stone wall before Jessie realized her mistake. Between the tree and the wall coming up, she should have swung wide, coming into the wall at an angle to make the rail beyond it possible. But she'd forgotten, and it was too late now. Trying to alter Spy's course would result in his running past the stone wall. Jessie's only hope was to slow him enough after landing so that she could turn him sharply and get him over the rails safely.

Spy cleared the stones with a foot to spare—his head up, his ears looking like two pieces of starched leather. Jessie could feel the violent energy pulsing through him. She checked him again with the reins, but he was finished listening to her. He had seen the rail already, and he obviously thought more of his jumping ability than Jessie did.

Paying no attention at all to Jessie's signals, Spy approached the rails at a terrible angle. He gathered himself and cleared the rail and stanchions in one tremendous leap. Jessie heard a sound like the wind. She only realized later that it must have been a collective gasp from the spectators who had gathered at the jump.

Forgetting her pride, forgetting everything but the necessity of staying on Spy's back, Jessie grabbed for Spy's mane. Her hands slipped off the tight nubs of braid, and she grabbed on to the saddle's pommel instead. They went over a hedge at a dead run. Then they were approaching the water obstacle, a shallow pond that the horses had to plow through to get to the remainder of the course.

The sight of the glistening water finally slowed Spy down, and the weight of the water against his legs slowed him even more. When they'd finished struggling up the bank on the opposite side, Jessie had regained a semblance of control.

A ditch—another stone wall—what could only be described as a rubbish heap—and Jessie had completed the course. She forced Spy into a circle after the last jump, checking him sharply with the reins and sitting well down in the saddle until she felt him paying attention to her. Then she turned him toward the finish and left the course at a controlled canter.

She could hear the cheers and whistles long before she got there. The announcer was giving her time and saying that there were no faults. Jessie hadn't paid particular attention to anyone else's time, but she was sure she had the fastest. She and Spy had done the course at breakneck speed. No one in their right mind would try to do it faster.

Kate and Dara, both mounted and waiting their turn, were standing in their stirrups, waving their hands above their heads like charging cavalry. Night Owl and Arpeggio danced excitedly under them.

"That was the most amazing course I've seen in years," said a tall blond man and he gave Jessie a big smile. "Best ride of the day!"

"Courageous is the word," said a woman next to him. "Heart. You had heart!"

Jessie tried to smile and nod her thanks. Her head was spinning and she was afraid that if she didn't get off Spy pretty soon she'd definitely pass out. *That* would certainly impress everyone!

She spotted Mr. Wiley in the crowd. He still looked completely amazed. Dismounting quickly, Jessie handed the reins to him.

"Jessie—" he began.

"I need to sit down," Jessie interrupted. Without waiting for his reply, she walked down the hill to the dressage arena and collapsed into the deserted judge's stand.

"I could have been killed out there," she told

the empty ring, "and they all thought it was wonderful!"

As her mind went over the ride she had just completed, Jessie felt more and more like smashing something. She had almost broken her neck in order to please her friends, and did they care? Were they even aware of it? No! They thought the whole thing was terrific!

Jessie had no idea how long she sat there. It took a long time before her heart stopped pounding and her anger ebbed. When she thought she could stand up again, she made her way back to the Wileys' van.

Kate and Dara were already there. "Where've you been?" Kate called.

"Getting my breath," Jessie said.

Dara and Kate were both grinning broadly. "That was a *fantastic* ride," Dara said.

"It must have been a blast," Kate added happily. "I'd have given my allowance for a year to have been on him."

Jessie looked at her friends in amazement. I knew it! she thought. They hadn't seen her danger. To them it looked like fun, something they would choose to do!

"Well, you've won the cross-country, too," Dara said. "One more to go."

One more? Jessie thought in panic. Oh yes, the stadium jumping. How could she go through with it? Dazed, she looked from Dara and Kate and then turned her eyes to Marc Wiley.

"Why don't we go get some refreshments?" he said to her. "You two stay here and guard the family fortune," he told Kate. "The champ and I are going to have a soda."

Marc put his arm around Jessie and led her away. "What's the matter, kiddo?" he asked gently.

Jessie looked up at him, and her eyes filled with tears. "They want me to do too much. I don't think I can ride again today," she said shakily.

"The outside course was a little too much for you?"

Jessie nodded.

"You handled it beautifully, though."

She swallowed. How could she tell him that *she* hadn't handled it at all?

"Spy's a dynamo," Mr. Wiley said. "But what grace, and class. You did a super job. I can see why the ride took a lot out of you." He paused. "However, I think you're treading on dangerous ground. If you don't get back on him, you'll take that shaky feeling home with you, and the next time you have to mount up it will be even harder.

"The last class is stadium jumping," he went on. "It's not a difficult course—four straightforward jumps set up in a circle. You go over them twice. You should have no trouble with Spy under those circumstances. Especially since you've already taken all he's got to offer and still managed him. I'm not going to push you into anything, but you've got your class won hands down. All you have to do is jump those four easy jumps and you've got yourself a well-earned blue ribbon, young lady. I'd hate to see you miss out on it because you're tired and a little unsure of yourself."

A little unsure of myself? Jessie looked up at Kate's father and wondered if there was anyone anywhere in the world who understood her.

Marc was smiling at her kindly. She looked away. Much as she hated to hear it, a lot of what he'd said was true. If she didn't get back up on Spy, the chances were that it would be harder and harder for her to find the courage to ride again. And the stadium-jumping class *was* a cinch. Spy would never have the chance to run away with her there.

They reached the refreshment stand, and Mr. Wiley bought them each a can of soda. Grateful, Jessie drank it. Suddenly it occurred to her that she hadn't even asked how Dara and Kate had done.

"They both had good rounds, but after your go, everything else was flat. I'll tell you the truth, Jessie. Kate's more excited about your getting a first than she is about anything she or Dara may do today."

Jessie finished the soda, dropped the can into the garbage pail, and turned to Mr. Wiley. "Guess we'd better get back," she said, and forced a smile. "I wouldn't want to disappoint Kate."

Mr. Wiley gave her an odd look. "Or yourself either, kiddo," he said.

Marc Wiley had been right. The stadium jumping was no problem. Jessie had a clean round. When the scores were in and averaged, she had indeed won the blue ribbon for the novice class.

"Totally unfair," muttered a thin, angry-looking blond woman next to Jessie and Kate. "What's a horse of his caliber doing competing as a novice at a schooling event? I can't believe these judges sometimes."

Jessie gave Kate an anxious glance. "Don't you worry, Jess," said Kate—just loud enough to be overheard. "That's just sour grapes." With a toss of her head the blond woman walked away, and Kate giggled.

Dara won the blue for the training-level class, and Kate came in a close second. The difference in their score came from the dressage class. Arpeggio had turned in a better performance than Night Owl.

"Well, I'm not crazy about it," Kate had said, trying not to sound upset, "but I have to admit you did ride a better test than I did, Dara. We'll just have to work harder," she said, running a hand down Night Owl's back.

"Let's get on the road, gang," Mr. Wiley said. "Your poor, crippled mom will be wanting to know what's happened."

"And Dara's got an important appointment," Kate said.

"And you've probably got another telephone call coming," Mr. Wiley said and grinned when Kate blushed.

"And I need two aspirins and a long, hot bath," Jessie muttered.

"I'll bet Sarah will be thrilled with the ribbon," Kate said, hugging her friend.

"She probably will be," Jessie agreed. It would be fun to tell her little sister about the day. For Sarah's benefit, Jessie would make it sound exciting instead of scary. Sarah was starting to show signs of interest in riding. One of the things Jessie had been looking forward to was putting Sarah up on Time-Out when the mare was ridable again. But that dream was gone too. There was no way in the world that she could put Sarah up on Spy.

"What have you got to look so glum about?" Kate said, seeing the expression on Jessie's face.

"Because—" Jessie began sharply. She stopped herself and softened her voice. "Because Dara's going home to a date, and you're going home to a telephone call, and I'm going home to a bath."

"But you're going home with a blue ribbon," Kate said. "That beats a telephone call or a date any day of the week."

The thing that amazed Jessie was that Kate really meant it.

Chapter 8

JESSIE pushed open the doors of the cafeteria and made her way to the table where the gang usually had lunch. They were all there. When they saw her coming, Bruce, Pete Hastings, and Amory stood up and whistled and clapped. Kate, Dara, Monica, and Kristin, the other members of the bunch, looked on smiling.

"What's that for?" Jessie asked.

"Let me shake the hand of the woman that shook the horse-world," her friend Bruce said solemnly, reaching over to pump her hand. "We heard you rode an outside course that may never be equaled."

"K-Kate told us you were really spectacular," Amory said, stammering a little. "That's really fantastic."

Jessie didn't say anything. Bruce ran a hand through his mop of red hair in mock bewilderment. "You'd think our heroine would have some kind of reaction to this reception," he said.

"She's overcome," Pete answered. "Give her a minute."

"I *am* overcome," Jessie said honestly. "Thank you, though."

"And," Kate said, "not that we don't appreciate praise from you guys, but Mr. Yon, the second greatest riding coach in the world—my mother being the first—called Miss Robeson from Florida to say that he'd had reports that she had ridden in a manner befitting Spy's talent and lineage."

"Word got all the way to Florida already?" Bruce said. He sounded really impressed.

"Who's Spy?" Amory asked.

"The horse I rode," Jessie answered Amory. She turned to Bruce. "Mr. Yon owns him. That's why word got to Florida."

"You didn't ride your own horse?" Amory asked, pushing his glasses up higher on his nose.

"I don't have a horse," Jessie said.

"Not yet," Kate said.

Jessie looked at her. "Not ever," she said.

"Don't be too sure of that." Kate grinned broadly. "I've got the greatest idea."

"What?" Jessie asked suspiciously.

"I think you ought to lease Spy."

"Lease Spy?" Jessie repeated dumbly.

"Sure. You should know by now that Mr. Yon is not exactly anxious to sell him. After your performance on Saturday, he'd probably be thrilled to have you ride him."

"Sounds like the perfect solution to me," Bruce said to Pete, "since these girls seem determined to fritter their time away on horseback. What do you think?"

"I'd go for it," Pete said. "Not that I know anything about it."

Jessie wished they would stop acting so silly. For a dozen reasons, leasing Spy was not something she wanted to joke about. "We couldn't afford it," she told Kate. That was the simplest one of those reasons.

"Oh, phooey," Kate said. "All you have to do is explain things to Mr. Yon. He'll come up with some arrangement—I just know it. Oh, Jessica Claire!" Kate said, giving Jessie a hug. "Imagine it. You, me, or Dara winning every event from now until October!"

"Nothing shy about our Katie," Kristin said to Monica, her brown eyes laughing.

"There's no sense in having false modesty," Kate said. "I learned that earlier this season. If you're good, flaunt it," she said, her eyes sparkling, "and we're good! So anyway, that's the plan. You lease Spy, and we set the eventing circuit on its ear."

"Kate," Jessie said patiently, "Mr. Yon doesn't know me from Cybill Shepherd. Why would he want to lease me his horse for practically nothing? —which is the only way I could afford it."

Bruce chuckled. "She's right there," he said to Pete. "Actually, Cybill Shepherd might have a better chance, her being on television and all."

"Will you two shut *up*?" Jessie flared. There was a sudden silence, and Jessie realized with embarrassment how angry she had sounded.

"All you have to do is call and ask him," Kate said to Jessie, her voice suddenly subdued.

"I can't," Jessie said.

"If you would stop being so neg—" Kate started, but Jessie interrupted her.

"I can't call him. Drop the subject. Please."

"Okay, okay," Kate said, puzzled. "Don't get all tied up in knots."

"Thank you," Jessie said.

"Can we get on with lunch now?" Monica asked.

"I think so," Kristin said, eyeing Kate and Jessie. "Today's installment of Horse and Rider seems to be over."

Jessie was quiet for the rest of the meal. She had a horrible feeling she'd said much too much already. And whenever Kate tried to catch her eye, she looked away.

Just before the bell rang, Doug Lyons walked over to their table. "Hi, guys," he said offhandedly.

Monica almost choked on her milk. "Hi, Doug!" she chirped perkily. "How's it going?"

"Fine, thanks," Doug answered. But he wasn't looking at Monica.

"Want to go outside?" he asked Dara.

She smiled. "Sure." And as Monica watched in stunned silence, Dara got up and left the cafeteria with Doug.

"Is she dating him?" Monica asked Kate, a note of awe in her voice.

"Looks like it," Kate said airily.

That's right, Jessie thought. Dara had gone out with Doug for the first time, and Jessie hadn't even asked her if she'd had fun! It looked as though things had gone quite well, but Jessie still wished she'd remembered to ask Dara about the date. I guess I've just been thinking too hard about my own problems, she told herself reproachfully.

"Well," Kate said, gathering up her lunch things, "I've got a test next period. I think I'll do some studying."

"Anyone for Frisbee?" Bruce asked, and Monica and Kristin both groaned.

"I see Frisbees in my sleep," Monica complained. "We've been playing it at every lunch for a month!"

"Think of something better to do, and I'll do it," Bruce challenged.

"Well ... okay," Monica said wearily, "let's play Frisbee. But I warn you, my days of flinging that pie plate around are numbered."

"Pie plate?" Bruce said to the bright orange Frisbee he'd just pulled out from under his chair. "Did you hear what she called you?"

"Coming?" Amory asked Jessie.

"No, you go ahead," Jessie said. "I want to get some dessert."

"Will I see you later at the barn?" Kate asked.

"Sure," Jessie said, not quite meeting her friend's eyes. "I mean, maybe."

Lease Spy. The words had been circling in Jessie's brain all afternoon, ever since Kate had first spoken them. Lease Spy. Jessie took a deep breath, looked out the school-bus window, and watched the stores of downtown Smithfield give way to houses.

Leasing Spy would mean she'd have to ride him ... a lot. Maybe that was good. Maybe she'd get to understand his moods better, and he'd be easier to control.

But she'd have to spend the rest of her life at the barn for that to happen, Jessie thought morosely. And she'd never get to do anything else—including seeing her family. It had been bad enough sacrificing so much of her social life to horses, but to sacrifice her family life, too ... Sarah sometimes talked wistfully about how little she saw Jessie. How would she feel if Jessie had to spend even more time away from home?

"We'll set the eventing circuit on its ear!" Kate had said. Jessie imagined the three of them piling up one blue ribbon after another. She'd hang them in Sarah's room, and the little girl would be thrilled. . . .

Then what was the matter with her? Why didn't Kate's idea fill her with joy? Why wasn't she jumping at the idea of calling Mr. Yon and seeing what could be arranged?

Because you're dumb! Jessie scolded herself, sitting up straighter in the bus seat. This is what you've said you wanted—a horse to ride and event. Now would you please stop being such a wet blanket about things?

When she got home, Jessie told herself sternly, she was going to hotfoot it over to the barn to exercise Spy—and show him who was boss. Then she was going to tell her dad about the idea. *Then* she'd call Mr. Yon and see what he said. Got that? she asked herself.

At least Kate would be happy. Jessie smiled slightly, imagining how pleased Kate would be tomorrow when Jessie casually told her, "By the way, I spoke to Mr. Yon last night, and he's working out the details of a lease." Kate would scream and hug her, and they'd dance around like two crazy people.

So that's that! Jessie told herself. It's settled.

"Doesn't someone get off at this stop?" asked the bus driver. Jessie looked out the window and saw her street. "Yes, me," she said, standing up so quickly that she almost dropped her books. "I was daydreaming. Sorry."

As Jessie turned into her drive, she was surprised to find Mrs. Mac waiting for her in the doorway with her coat on.

"Jessie, love, I'm glad you're home," said Mrs. Mac breathlessly. "The volunteer who usually drives Mr. McPhaden for his physical therapy can't make it, and I'm going to have to take him. Can you stay home for Sarah? Nick has Little League this afternoon and then he's going to have dinner with the Mardons, so you don't have to worry about him."

"Sure," Jessie said after a second. What else could she do?

"Were you going to the barn today?" Mrs. Mac asked, her gray eyes warm with concern.

"Yes, but that doesn't matter. You go ahead."

"Jessie, I wouldn't do this to you—I know how much you enjoy riding—but I have no choice. I'm going to be late as it is."

"That's okay, honestly," Jessie said, bending to kiss Mrs. Mac on the cheek. "You go ahead. I can handle the afternoon, and we'll see you tomorrow. You can make it up to me by baking some more of your double-chocolate-chip cookies."

Mrs. MacPhaden gave Jessie a quick hug. "I already have. And there's a casserole in the fridge for dinner," she added over her shoulder. "Thank you, honey."

Jessie walked into the quiet house and closed the door behind her. So much for her plans.

She plopped her books down on the kitchen table, grabbed some cookies and a glass of milk, and sat down. The whole afternoon stretched in front of her. She glanced at the clock. Sarah would be home in forty-five minutes. Maybe she'd take her over to the park and they could both ride on the swings. That would be a lot of fun, actually. They hadn't done that for a long time.

Right after she finished her snack, she'd go upstairs, put on her old jeans, and wait for Sarah on the front steps. She was already looking forward to the little girl's delight when she found Jessie waiting for her.

Jessie kept waiting to start resenting the fact that she wouldn't be able to ride this afternoon. But it didn't happen. She didn't feel resentful at all. What she really felt was relieved.

The park was filled with the sounds of children of all ages. There were two baseball games going on—one of them starring Nicholas Robeson—and there was a game of tag and one of hide-and-seek. Jessie and Sarah were sitting on the swings, rocking gently as they watched the activity.

They'd been there for over an hour, and Jessie could tell by Sarah's fidgeting that she was ready for something new. "Let's go see the horses," Sarah said suddenly.

"You mean at Kate's?"

"Uh-huh," Sarah said. "You told me that when I was bigger you'd show me how to ride. Am I big enough yet?" she asked hopefully.

"You're getting there," Jessie said. She didn't want to dash her sister's hopes by telling her the horse she'd had in mind for the lessons wasn't available anymore.

"Let's go see them," Sarah insisted. "Maybe when we get there I'll be big enough. And anyway, you haven't shown me the baby yet."

"Okay, Sarah. You'll have to ride in the kiddie

seat on my bike, though," Jessie warned, "and sit very still."

Sarah nodded her agreement. The sisters walked back to the house, clamped the seat onto Jessie's bike, and then set off for Windcroft.

Dara's car was parked in the drive when they got there, but there was no sign of either Kate or Dara. They must be out on a trail ride, Jessie thought.

She took Sarah's hand and led her toward the paddock. Jonathan, Kate's mother's horse, and Northern Spy were together in one field. Jessie sat Sarah on the fence and stood behind her. The horses eyed them, uncertain what they were there for. In a minute Jonathan went back to grazing, but Spy continued to stare.

"What's he looking at?" Sarah asked nervously.

"He's trying to decide if we've come to stop his fun," Jessie said.

Spy took several steps toward them, his head raised, sniffing the air. Then he lowered his head, pawed the ground, and whirled to nip Jonathan in the flanks. Jonathan kicked playfully at him. Spy reared a little, then took off for the far corner of the field, his mane and tail flowing out behind him.

"That's the horse I rode in the competition. Isn't he magnificent?" Jessie asked her sister softly.

"No," Sarah said. "He's scary. Where's your other horse?"

"Time-Out?"

"Uh-huh," Sarah said. "That's the one I like. Let's go see him."

"Her," Jessie corrected, lifting Sarah down from the fence. "She's over here."

Jessie led her sister to a small exercise area on
the far side of the barn. The door to Time-Out's
foaling stall opened directly into it. The mare was
inside the stall, standing quietly, her head hanging over the sleeping form of her colt.

"See the baby?" Jessie asked. Sarah nodded,
entranced.

Jessie whistled softly, and Time-Out's ears
perked up as she turned to look at her. "Hi,
sweetie pie!" Jessie said. The mare whinnied and
walked slowly toward them.

Sarah climbed up on the fence, delighted. When
Time-Out reached them, Jessie scratched the mare
behind the ears. Time-Out walked forward so that
her head was over Jessie's shoulder. She'd always
done that with Jessie. Jessie figured it was as
close to a hug as a horse could give.

Sarah tentatively reached out a hand and stroked
the mare's warm neck. "I like this horse, Jessie,"
Sarah said.

"Me, too," Jessie told her.

"Am I big enough to ride her?" Sarah asked.
"Please? You promised."

"What do you think, Time-Out? Is Sarah big
enough?"

As if she understood exactly what Jessie had
said, Time-Out nodded her head.

"She said yes!" Sarah said excitedly.

"Then I guess it's all right." Jessie hopped over
the fence and lifted Sarah onto the mare's back.
"Hold on to her mane," Jessie said.

Jessie held Time-Out's halter and led her around
the edge of the paddock, Sarah sitting proud as a
princess on the horse's back. When they came
back to where they'd started, Jessie reached out

to help Sarah down. But Sarah ignored her and leaned forward to stretch her arms as far as they would go around Time-Out's neck. "I love you, horse," she said, and kissed Time-Out's smooth brown hair.

"I love you, too, horse," Jessie said—and she looked away so that Sarah wouldn't see the stupid tears in her eyes.

Sarah talked nonstop about her first "horse lesson" all through supper. Mr. Robeson listened with a smile. But after they had finished eating and he and Jessie were doing the dishes, he said dejectedly, "I'm going to have to look for another housekeeper, Jessie. I can't have your life interrupted all the time, much as Sarah would love it."

"Oh, Dad—" Jessie began unhappily.

"I know," her father said. "The idea doesn't thrill me either. Mrs. Mac is a gem. But I can't have you responsible for the kids. After your success this weekend, you're going to want to spend more time at the barn, not less."

"I guess so. Mr. Yon called the Wileys," Jessie told him. "He's the one who owns the horse I rode. He said people had been calling to tell him what a good job I did."

"I'm not surprised," Mr. Robeson said proudly. "I know what you're capable of."

"Kate thinks there's a chance that Mr. Yon might let me lease Spy without it costing too much."

"Wouldn't that be wonderful?" her father said.

"Do you think it's a good idea?"

"It sounds like it. Isn't it what you want, a horse to ride? I only wish we could buy him for you, honey."

"I know, Daddy," Jessie said quickly. "I know you're doing as much as you can for me. I don't think I want to own him, anyway."

"Why not?" her father asked, rinsing the last dish and handing it to Jessie.

Jessie shrugged. "I don't know. But anyway, Kate thinks Mr. Yon will be so pleased to have me ride Spy that he'll jump at the chance of my leasing him. He doesn't really seem to want to sell Spy."

"That's odd, isn't it?" Mr. Robeson asked.

"A little. I don't get it, myself."

"Well, if you can work it out," said her father, "you've got my blessing. In the meantime I'll call some agencies and see what they have in the way of housekeepers."

Jessie looked quickly over at her father. She could see by his expression that he was thinking the same thing she was. They'd have a hard time finding anyone as perfect for them as Mrs. Mac.

She finished drying the dishes, wiped off the counter, and hung the towel up to dry.

Kate thought leasing Spy was a good idea. Jessie's father thought it was a good idea. With a little time to get used to it, maybe she'd think it was a good idea, too.

Chapter 9

"JESSIE, Jessie, wait up!"

Jessie turned to see Dara making her way through the morning crowd in the hallway of Smithfield Regional High.

"Where's Kate?" Dara asked as the two girls headed toward their first-period class. "I didn't see her at her locker."

"I don't know," Jessie said. "Maybe she's sick."

"I don't think so. She was fine yesterday. She's probably goofing off."

"Kate?" Jessie said, her eyebrows raised.

"Not likely?" Dara asked.

"Not likely," Jessie agreed. "She's got to be around somewhere. You're looking very happy these days," she added.

"I am." Dara grinned broadly.

"Does it have anything to do with a certain guy who shall remain nameless?"

"Mmmm," Dara said, still grinning.

"Are you two really dating?" Jessie asked. "Monica's having a fit, you know."

"I guess we really are," Dara said. "We went out Saturday night after the show, and then he came over on Sunday and we just hung around and listened to music, and he called me last night and I'm supposed to meet him after lunch."

"Sounds pretty serious to me," Jessie said, wondering how it could have happened so fast. Dara had only been in Smithfield two months, and already she'd snared the most popular guy in school. "Did you date a lot in Pennsylvania?" she asked her friend.

"No. There was a group of us, kind of like the lunch bunch here, and when anything happened we all showed up together. But there wasn't any one guy I was interested in," Dara said.

Jessie looked over at Dara's smooth blond hair, perfect skin, and summer-blue eyes. Maybe Dara hadn't been interested in anyone, but Jessie was sure there'd been a dozen guys who had been interested in her.

"I wasn't ready to date in Pennsylvania," Dara continued. "But I am now. Doug is really terrific. You'd think he might be stuck on himself, but he isn't. The thing I like the best about him is that he doesn't play mind games. I mean, I don't have to pretend to be hard to get, or tell a lot of dumb lies. I can just be myself." She paused a minute and smiled ruefully. "You might find this hard to believe, but the real me isn't easy for some people to take."

"Well, you *are* pretty straightforward," Jessie said. "I mean, you definitely have opinions, and you're not shy about stating them."

"Some people have problems with that," Dara said.

"But not Doug?"

"Not Doug. At least not yet."

"Well, here we are," Jessie said, looking gloomily at the open door to their English lit class.

"Courage," Dara said. "A few more weeks and final exams, and then a whole summer to relax in. By the way—talking about summer, I'm thinking about spending some time at a riding camp in Vermont. It's run by Tommy Langwald."

"Didn't he compete in combined training events in the Olympics?" Jessie asked as they walked toward their desks.

"Yeah. He was great. I think we could learn a lot from him. I'm going to mention it to Kate, too. Don't you think it would be super if we all went?"

"Girls," their teacher Mrs. Dardenne said, "take your seats, please. The bell's about to ring." As if on cue, the bell did ring, and Mrs. Dardenne closed the door behind them.

Kate still hadn't arrived. But halfway through the hour, the door opened and she came in with a late pass. She was radiant with happiness about something. *What happened?* Jessie telegraphed with her eyes. But Kate wasn't paying attention. She sat down, shut her eyes tight, and smiled again.

"Miss Wiley? Miss Robeson? Are we done making faces at each other?" asked Mrs. Dardenne.

Jessie turned around quickly. "Sorry," she mumbled. What in the world was going on with Kate? She looked like the cat that swallowed the canary! It was obvious she was dying to tell Jessie something. Maybe Pete had finally gotten around to asking the big question again. Well, it would have to wait until class was over.

As it turned out, Jessie had to wait until lunchtime to find out. Mrs. Dardenne kept Kate after class to fill her in on what she had missed. When Jessie arrived at their usual lunch table, Kate was waiting for her. "Thank heavens you're here!" Kate said, bouncing in her seat. "I don't think I can keep this to myself one minute more. Do you know why I was late this morning?"

"You tried putting on those fake lashes again?" Jessie asked.

"*Very* funny," Kate said. Jessie had never let her forget the time she had gotten a fake eyelash stuck half on and half off her eyelid. "I was late because I had to make a telephone call." She waited for a second, but Jessie didn't say anything. "Ask me who I had to call!" Kate squealed.

"Who?"

"Mr. Yon," Kate answered, and smiled conspiratorially at Jessie.

A funny feeling began to stir inside Jessie. "And?" she asked.

"And ... you can have Spy!"

Jessie just stared at her.

"Did you hear me?" Kate asked. "You can lease him! At next to nothing!"

"Mr. Yon called last night to talk to Mom about something," Kate rushed on, "and I just happened to answer the phone—and I just happened to mention the possibility of your leasing Spy. Then Mom got on and said what a great person you were, and that my dad had said you rode Spy like a pro, and what did Mr. Yon think of my idea? And then I got back on and told him that he'd have to come up with generous terms because you guys aren't rich, and wouldn't it be worth it to have Spy being taken care of by someone like Jessica Claire Robeson? Then he said he had to think it over and Mom should call him this morning," Kate stopped to take a breath. "But Mom had to go to the doctor, so I stayed home and called him, and he said yes! And wait until you hear the terms!" she finished exultantly.

"What's all the hollering about?" Dara asked, setting her tray down next to Jessie. She looked from the wide-eyed Jessie to the equally wide-eyed Kate. "What gives, you guys?"

"Mr. Yon is going to lease Spy to Jessie. That means a whole summer of eventing—and better yet, winning—for the three of us."

"Wow," Dara said slowly. "How'd you manage that?"

"It was easy," Kate said. "I asked him. Jessie, we can start really training this afternoon! Just think of it—hours, weeks, months of riding Northern Spy ahead of you."

"I wish you had asked me about this first," Jessie said slowly.

"I did ask you," Kate said. "At lunch. Remember we talked about it?"

"And I told you to drop the subject," Jessie answered. "Why don't you ever listen to me?"

"Jessie!" Kate said. She sounded stunned. "I did listen. You said you didn't know Mr. Yon well enough to talk to him, so I did."

"You had no right to do that!"

"What is the matter with you?" Kate asked, her voice rising. "I've just done you the biggest favor in the world—and you're mad. You're always mad, Jessie. Have you noticed that?"

"Maybe it's because people keep planning my life for me."

"Is that supposed to mean me?"

"Yes," Jessie snapped.

"Hey, guys!" Dara said. "Cool down! This is getting out of hand."

"Why?" Jessie asked. "Because for once I'm not going along with Kate's interference?"

"Interference!" Kate shouted. "I like that. I missed half of first period for you and Mrs. Dardenne is making me do extra homework that I don't have time for. And you're mad at me?"

"Kate! Jessie!" Dara said again. "Everyone's staring at you!"

Jessie looked from Dara to Kate. Her face was flushed, her eyes furious. "Stop pushing me," she said in a low voice. "Okay? Just stop pushing me!" She jumped up from the table. If she stayed there one more minute, she was either going to burst into tears or say something she'd never be able to take back.

She pushed her way out of the cafeteria and ran blindly down the hall. At the end of the hall, the door to an empty study room stood open. Jessie walked in, collapsed into a chair, and closed her eyes.

"Jessie?"

She looked toward the doorway to find Dara standing there.

"What?" she asked, looking away again as Dara came in and sat down next to her. "I guess I made a total fool of myself," Jessie said.

"I don't know if I'd put it in quite those words," Dara said. "It certainly was a switch from the way you usually act."

"I'd just as soon not talk about it," Jessie said, her voice hard. "Do you mind?"

"I think that's a mistake," Dara said calmly. "Obviously you're pretty teed off about something. When you're upset, it's a good thing to get it out in the open. What got you going?"

Jessie sat forward with her head in her hands. "I never said I wanted to lease Spy," she said in a muffled voice.

"You never said you didn't," Dara said.

"I told Kate to drop the subject," Jessie retorted.

"Yeah, but *we* thought it was because *you* thought you couldn't afford it. That wasn't it?"

"No, that wasn't it. Look," Jessie said, sitting back and turning to face Dara. "I'm a nervous wreck most of the time I'm on Spy's back." She held up a hand to stop Dara from interrupting. "I know what you're going to say—if I ride him longer, I'll feel more secure. To some extent that's true. But there's more. I don't know how to say this. I don't want the responsibility of a horse like Spy.

"I mean, he's something special," she went on. "He deserves to have someone ride him who's willing to put in the time and effort to be as good as he can be. He needs a better match then me." Did Dara understand all this? "I'm not as competitive as you and Kate are," Jessie said. "It isn't important to me that I come in first, that my horse be the best. I like things a little slower. I like to do things at my own pace, not because it's important to score high at the next event. Spy—Spy should have more than that," she finished.

"Spy should have Kate," Dara said softly.

The words stopped Jessie cold. She stared at Dara. "But Kate has Night Owl!"

Dara shook her head. "Kate's all the things you said you're not," she said. "She's competitive, and willing to work hard to get where she wants to go. But she's not going to get there on Night Owl. He's wonderful, and dear, and I know she loves him—but he's just not talented enough to make it at the higher levels of competition. Even Arpeggio's beating him—and Arpeggio's good, but he's not spectacular."

"And Spy is," Jessie said softly. She was still for a minute, remembering the expression on Mr. Yon's face when he'd learned it would be Jessie riding Spy, not Kate. "Do you think that's what Mr. Yon had in mind all the time? Do you think that's why he wouldn't sell Spy and finagled him into Windcroft?"

"It's possible," Dara said. "Everybody says what a devious old guy he is."

"That *would* make sense, wouldn't it?" Jessie said, leaning back in her chair.

"To everyone but Kate." Dara smiled.

"Kate," Jessie whispered. "I said some awful things to her." She sighed. "Kate and her mom and Mr. Yon, they've all gone out of their way to be nice to me. And I end up by shouting at Kate. She must think I'm the most ungrateful person in the world."

"Kate's your friend, Jessie. All she was trying to do was make you happy."

"Maybe it's not possible for me to be happy.

Maybe I'm the kind of person that's just naturally miserable."

"Maybe you're the kind of person who hasn't taken the time to figure out what it is that will make you happy."

"I guess I owe Kate an apology," Jessie said.

"And an explanation," Dara said.

"And an explanation," Jessie repeated, staring down at her hands. "You know, until just now, talking to you, I didn't realize how I really felt."

"You have to take time to decide what it is you want. You have to set your own goals. If you don't, you end up being part of somebody else's, and that's no good. Even if that somebody else thinks they're doing you a favor."

"Like Kate," Jessie said. The wall clock clicked loudly as the hands reached half-past the hour. Jessie glanced up. "I've made you miss lunch," she said.

"That's okay, but you're not going to make me miss Doug," Dara said, standing up. "That's one of *my* goals." She grinned at Jessie.

Jessie smiled back. "Thanks, Dara," she said.

"See you today at the barn?"

Jessie looked at her a long minute, then slowly nodded her head.

Kate was mucking out stalls when Jessie arrived at Windcroft. "Hi," Jessie said from the doorway.

"Hi," Kate said quietly, without looking up.

"I'm sorry for the way I blew up at you today."

Kate jammed the pitchfork she was using down into the bedding and turned to face Jessie. "Would you like to tell me what all that was about?" Her blue-gray eyes were filled with tears.

Jessie walked into the dim barn. "Dara didn't say anything to you?"

"I haven't seen Dara since she took off after you at lunch," Kate said.

"Then you probably think I'm a first-class jerk," Jessie said miserably.

"Jessie, you're my friend. Just tell me what's wrong."

"It's hard for me to do that," Jessie said. "I've kept everything to myself for so long that it's hard to put my feelings into words."

Kate leaned the pitchfork against the stall and came to sit on the doorstep where Jessie was standing. She shielded her eyes against the bright glare of the sun and stared up at Jessie.

"Try," she said.

Jessie sat down beside her. "I don't want you to think I don't appreciate what you did," she began slowly. "When I got home from school yesterday, I had just about talked myself into thinking you were right. I even told my dad about your plan, and he said if we could work it out I should go for it. But I wasn't being truthful with anyone, not even myself, because down deep inside I really don't want Spy." In a rush of words she went on to tell Kate what she had already told Dara.

Kate listened carefully. "Are you sure you're just not afraid to let yourself want him?" she asked when Jessie was done.

"Kate, it's taken me a long time to really understand and admit how I feel! Don't go looking for ways to explain it that are more to your liking!"

"Do I do that?" Kate asked.

"Sometimes. And I'm not always strong enough to stand up to you when you're doing it."

Kate drew a little circle in the dust with the toe of her boot. "Well, okay," she finally said. "It's no big deal. I'll tell Mr. Yon that I was mistaken."

She looked at Jessie inquiringly, as if waiting for her to have a change of heart. When Jessie didn't say anything, Kate dropped her eyes. "But if you don't lease Spy, then what?" she asked.

"I don't know." Jessie sighed. "I guess that's the other reason I let things get so out of hand. You've been my best friend since junior high school. I can't stand the thought of not doing things with you." She looked at Kate and gave her a small smile. "I kind of understand how Pete must feel. You're all tied up in horses, and if I don't have a horse, I'll probably see you about as often as he does."

"Don't be silly," Kate said. "There's more to our friendship than horses—I hope."

"I hope so, too," said Jessie. "But you have to admit that riding's pretty much all you guys do."

"Yeah." There was a little silence. "If you don't want what I want," Kate said, studying her friend, "what *do* you want?"

"Well, I want some of the things that you want. I do want to ride, and I do want a horse. Is that enough of a goal?"

Kate thought about it for a minute. "Nope," she said. "Too general. You have to be more specific."

"Okay, then. I want a nice, friendly, fun-to-ride horse. One that I can let Sarah get on, and maybe teach her how to ride someday."

"Like Time-Out," Kate said, and Jessie nodded. The girls were quiet. Above them, swallows swooped in and out of the open hay-loading door in the loft of the barn. The sun was warm on Jessie's legs.

"Jessie," Kate said slowly.

"What?" Jessie asked.

"Why not want Time-Out?" Kate said, then turned to face Jessie. "Why not?" she asked again. A familiar note of excitement was creeping into her words. "Mrs. Jesper said they were thinking of selling her. You could call Mrs. Jesper and . . ."

Kate's words slowed, and she fell silent. "I'm doing it again, aren't I? I'm pushing."

Jessie grinned. "I don't think you can help it," she said.

"I can't, Jessie. Honest to goodness, I can't. I want so much for you to be happy again."

"Then we're still friends?" Jessie said.

"We never weren't," Kate said. "Now, I'm going to say one more thing, and then I swear I'll never bring the subject up again. I can see by your face that you're about to say, 'Mrs. Jesper would never sell Time-Out to me.' But remember, you also said that there was no way you could ever lease Spy—and you were wrong there. So don't just shrug your shoulders and say there's no way. Setting a goal is only the first step. The second step is finding a way to make it happen."

Kate stared intently at Jessie and then dropped her eyes. "That's all I'm going to say," she promised. Then she reached over to give Jessie a hug. "I'm so glad you came over this afternoon. I was afraid we wouldn't be able to patch things up today and I'd have nightmares about your never talking to me again."

"You'd have nightmares about our not being friends?" Jessie asked in wonder.

"Of course! Wouldn't you?"

"Kate, if things don't work out, and I don't ever have another horse to ride, how will we *stay* friends?"

"I have no idea. All I can tell you is that somehow we will. And now that we've straightened things out, I've got to get busy." Kate scrambled to her feet. "I've got to finish mucking the stalls, then take the Owl into the ring and go over some jumps. And then I guess I'll have to exercise Spy, too."

"Kate, I'm sorry. My not riding Spy is going to make extra work for you, isn't it?"

"Don't be sorry. To tell you the truth, I was looking for an excuse to ride him. He's such a handful that it'll be fun."

"Then the least I can do is muck the stalls for you," Jessie said. And, refusing to listen to Kate's objections, she picked up the pitchfork.

Jessie did all of the stalls. It was time-consuming and hard, but when she was finished she felt as if she'd paid Kate back a little for today. After she'd put the pitchfork away, she went into the tack room and fished a can of soda out of the cooler. She popped the top, took a long, refreshing swallow of root beer, and walked to the doorway.

Kate was riding Northern Spy in the ring. Jessie watched while they circled the ring—first at a trot, then at a spirited canter. Kate turned the horse toward the jumps and Spy took each of them in turn, smoothly as silk. They made a beautiful picture.

Jessie kept thinking about what Dara had said.

The more she thought about it, the more sense it made. Mr. Yon had meant Spy for Kate, but Kate didn't realize it yet. And when Kate did realize it, Jessie didn't think it would make her happy. Kate loved Night Owl. It was going to hurt her a lot that Night Owl couldn't be the horse to take her to the top. Well, Jessie thought, I'll try to help Kate as much as she's helped me.

Jessie dropped the empty soda can into the trash bag and walked slowly to the back of the barn where Time-Out and her colt were kept. But the stall and paddock were empty. She searched the field until she finally saw them on the other side of the small creek that divided the Windcroft field in half.

Jessie stared at them for a long time. I wonder ... she thought before picking up her bike, waving good-bye to Kate, and heading for home.

Chapter 10

THAT night Jessie dreamed she was riding across a never-ending green meadow. Next to her, on a miniature horse, was Sarah. "I like this, Jess," Sarah said. "I like this a lot."

"Want to go faster?" Jessie asked, squeezing her legs against Time-Out. The mare increased her pace, checking back over her shoulder occasionally to be sure that Sarah and the colt were keeping up.

"We won't let anything happen to them, will we?" Jessie whispered to the mare.

"I'm not scared at all," Sarah said happily.

"Neither am I," Jessie agreed.

"Can we do this again tomorrow?" Sarah asked.

"No," Jessie said. "We can't ever do this again."

"But I want to!" Sarah wailed.

"Well, we can't," Jessie said sharply.

"We could if you would set your goals," Sarah told her. Jessie turned quickly to look at her little sister—and found she was looking instead at Kate.

Kate's knees were pulled up to her chin so that she could fit on the tiny horse.

"You promised not to keep after me!" Jessie told her. "You promised!"

Jessie woke with a start and lay in bed staring at her night table. The clock said 3 A.M. As she thought about the dream, she had to laugh. Kate was even haunting her sleep!

"Set your goals, set your goals," Jessie said aloud, throwing back her covers and sitting on the edge of her bed. "Easy for Kate Wiley, easy for Dara Cooper, hard for Jessie Robeson."

The curtain at her window moved gently in the night air. Jessie got up and went to look outside. The moon was full, and the trees and grass had a silver look, almost as if they'd been dusted by a snowfall. But it was early June, so that wasn't likely—not even in New England. What they'd been dusted by was moonlight.

The sky was bright with stars. Jessie wondered which one it was that Kate always wished on. Things happened for Kate and when they did, she'd smile and say, "I asked my lucky star." It must be a super-special star, because Kate got what she wished for almost all the time. Jessie had always been amazed at her friend's good luck. Maybe she got my share, she thought, running her fingers lightly along the window frame.

Or maybe it wasn't luck at all. Maybe Kate practiced what she preached. Maybe it was Jessie, not Kate who didn't listen.

Set goals, Kate had said. . . .

"All right." Jessie turned from the window angrily and faced her reflection in her dresser mirror. "My goal is to own Time-Out. See any way of that happening? No? I didn't think so."

She stomped back across the room and got into bed. "Obviously I'm setting the wrong goal." She pulled the sheet up over her head. "The goal I should set is to forget about riding completely."

She tossed fitfully for the rest of the night. When her alarm went off, she got up fuzzy-headed and out of sorts.

"A penny for your thoughts," her father said as he pulled the eggs and butter out of the refrigerator.

"They're not even worth that much," Jessie said. Groggily, she began to set the table for breakfast.

"Are Nick and Sarah up?" her father asked.

"Sarah's making her bed, and Nick is still in his. I've called him twice, and twice he's said he's getting up. Short of pulling him up physically, I don't know what else to do."

"Crack these eggs," Mr. Robeson said, handing Jessie the carton. He walked to the hallway connecting the kitchen with the bedrooms and called, "Nicholas! This is your commanding officer. On your feet!"

There was a moment of silence, then the sound of a door opening. "Why didn't someone call me?" a sleepy voice protested. "Now I'm going to be late."

"Nicholas—" Jessie began, but her father held up his hand to silence her. "For the sake of morning peace, let it pass," he said.

Sarah came scampering into the kitchen and climbed up on her chair. "For show-and-tell today, I want to bring Jessie's blue ribbon to school," she chattered. "Is that okay with you, Jessie?"

"It's yours, Sarah. I gave it to you."

"That's very generous," Mr. Robeson said, pouring orange juice for Sarah.

"Oh, she's going to get lots more," Sarah said.

"Don't count on it," Jessie said morosely. She spooned the eggs into the dishes and plunked herself down at the table.

"False modesty," Mr. Robeson commented.

"What's that mean?" Sarah asked, her mouth full of eggs.

"Don't talk with your mouth full!" Jessie said.

"If I don't talk while I'm eating, I'll never get to say anything to Daddy," Sarah complained. "Almost the only time I see him is at meals!"

Jessie started to say something, but then she caught her father's eye. "I know," she groaned, "for the sake of morning peace, I'll keep my mouth closed."

Nick came to the table, still stuffing his shirt into his jeans. He drank his orange juice before he sat down, then cleaned his plate in a matter of seconds. He took a swallow of his milk, wiped his mouth, and headed for the door.

"Slow down," Mr. Robeson told his son, "aren't you going to wait for Sarah?"

"Can't, Dad," Nick said. "The guys play baseball before school starts and if I don't get there fast I'll only get one turn up at bat."

"I'm ready anyways," Sarah said. Quickly she slipped off her chair and circled the table to kiss her father and Jessie good-bye.

"Hurry up!" Nick called from the hallway.

"Nick says I can be a cheerleader for the team," Sarah confided to Jessie as she hurried after her brother.

"A cheerleader? Our Sarah?" Mr. Robeson said when the front door had closed behind his younger children. "It boggles the mind." He sighed. "They both forgot to brush their teeth."

Jessie grinned halfheartedly. Gordon Robeson reached behind him for the coffeepot, poured himself another cup, and said, "Okay, out with it."

"Out with what?" Jessie said.

"With whatever's bothering you."

"Nothing's bothering me, Dad." Jessie forced herself to sound cheerful.

"Don't give me that 'nothing's bothering me' business anymore!" her father said sternly. Jessie could only stare at him. "I've been letting you say it, and accepting it, for far too long," her father said more quietly. "I'm finished with being shut out of your life—because, whether you realize it or not, that's what you're doing.

"I realize I'm partly to blame for the fact that we don't share much anymore," he continued. "For a long time I really wasn't ready to handle much more than what was happening to your mother. But that's over now. I think we're all ready to move ahead."

"Honestly, Dad," Jessie said, squirming in her chair, "there's nothing to tell!"

"Well," her father said, leaning back in his chair, "it's going to be a long morning, because neither one of us leaves this kitchen until you tell me what's got you looking so down in the mouth. Was Kate wrong? Is Mr. Yon not willing to lease that horse at a price we can afford?"

Jessie pushed her eggs back and forth across her plate. She couldn't look at her father. "It's going to sound so stupid after all the fuss I made about Spy to begin with."

"I'm in the mood for stupid stories," her father said and grinned. "Shoot."

So Jessie told him everything. She began with

how she'd felt when she lost the opportunity to ride Time-Out and went on through the fact that the Jespers were going to move and either take Time-Out with them or sell her. She told her father all about her brief, anxiety-ridden career with Spy, and ended with the argument and talk she'd had with Kate. And how Kate had insisted that the only way to get ahead in life was to know what you wanted and find a way to make it happen.

When she was finished, Jessie waited for her father to say something—but he didn't.

Anxiously Jessie went on, "I know it's impossible. I know we don't have the kind of money to buy a horse right now, and I understand, Dad, really I do. That's why I didn't want to get into all this."

"What is it that you really want?" her father asked softly.

"I want Time-Out."

"Is she for sale?"

"Not really. But maybe I could talk Mrs. Jesper into letting me buy her. It would be so right for everyone. Even for Time-Out," Jessie said. "Because Mrs. Jesper doesn't love her the way I do. Nobody would."

Mr. Robeson got up and walked slowly to the window. Then he turned and asked, "Assuming you could talk Mrs. Jesper into the sale, how much would a horse like Time-Out cost?"

Jessie was afraid to tell him, but at last she muttered the amount she guessed Mrs. Jesper would ask.

Her father didn't seem as horrified as she had expected. "You know," he said, "that's about the amount of money Gran gave me to put away for our big vacation—whenever we get around to taking it. But as far as I know, none of us is anxious to take any vacation at the moment. So what if we used the money to buy a horse?"

"I couldn't do that!" Jessie gasped. "Gran meant that money for all of us!"

"Gran meant for that money to give us a lift," her father answered. "She just mentioned a trip because that's what she likes to do. Of course, you couldn't use all of it. We'd have to save some for our excursions to Shea Stadium and the zoo. But even after those two big expenses there should be enough left over for a horse."

Jessie couldn't speak. All she could do was stare at her father.

"Smile, Jessie," he said, putting his hands on his daughter's shoulders. "It's time to be happy again ... time for all of us."

An hour later Jessie found Kate and Dara standing at Kate's locker.

"What's up?" Kate asked. "You look sort of funny."

"I *feel* funny." Jessie told her. "This making-goals business is scary."

"What happened?" Dara asked, and Jessie repeated the conversation she'd had with her father.

Before she was halfway through, Kate was dancing around her. "That's wonderful! That's wonderful!" she shrieked.

"But it's only the beginning," Jessie reminded her. "Now we have to convince Mrs. Jesper to sell Time-Out to me."

"True," Kate said, growing immediately serious. "Well, that's too complicated to try and deal with in school. Let's go to the mall tonight and map out our strategy."

"Good," Dara said. "Hot fudge always makes my mind work faster. I'll pick you guys up at seven-thirty."

At eight o'clock the girls trooped into the Lickety-Split Ice Cream Parlor at the mall and sat down in a booth. The mall was quieter than it would be on the weekend, and the Lickety-Split was almost empty. Amory waved at them, grabbed his order pad, and came over.

"Let's see," he said, "Three sundaes. Hot fudge sauce, buttercrunch ice cream, double whipped cream."

"Right," Dara said.

"Wrong," Jessie told her.

"Wrong?" Dara and Kate chorused.

"I'm not crazy about buttercrunch. I'd rather have chocolate chip mint ice cream."

"How come you never said anything about that before?" Kate asked her.

"It seemed silly to make a fuss over ice cream," Jessie answered.

"I wonder what else we've been doing that she doesn't like?" Dara said.

"I'll let you know when the next thing comes up," Jessie said, and grinned.

"Do you get the feeling we've created a monster?" Kate asked Dara.

"If you have, she's a really cool one." And then—as if he couldn't believe he had said the words—Amory blushed to the roots of his hair. "Two buttercrunch, one chocolate chip mint," he muttered quickly, and hurried back to the safety of the counter.

Kate stared first at Dara, then at Jessie. "I *told* you he likes you," she said to Jessie.

"That's another night's discussion, though," Dara said. "Tonight we're here on horse business."

They talked for almost two hours—hardly noticing when Amory slid the sundaes onto their table, hardly noticing when they had finished them. They discussed the best way, time, and place to approach Mrs. Jesper. They examined the best possible way to bring the subject up; they thought up an answer to every reason Mrs. Jesper might give Jessie for not selling Time-Out. They planned until they were exhausted.

"I think that's it," Kate said when neither Dara nor Jessie could think of a situation they hadn't considered.

"Good," Dara said, "because I've still got two hours of homework ahead of me."

"And I have to write an essay on the poem I missed in English," Kate said.

"There *is* one other thing," Jessie said. Kate groaned and laid her head down on the table. "If Mrs. Jesper says yes, then we have to come up with some way for me to repay at least part of the money to my dad."

"I thought you said it was a gift from your grandmother?" Kate asked, looking up.

"It is, but it's a gift to the whole family, not just me."

"Okay, but we don't have to get into that tonight. Right?" Kate asked.

"Right," Jessie answered.

"Now, you've got all the things we told you straight?" Dara asked Jessie.

"I've got so many questions and answers jammed

into my head, I'm surprised my skinny old neck can still support it." Jessie clamped her hands around her throat.

"When you get home," Kate told her, "drink a glass of warm milk, go upstairs, lie down on your bed with the light off, and just let everything we talked about tonight float through your head. That's what I do when I've studied for a test for as long as I can stand it. You'll be surprised how much you've retained."

"Then let's get going," Jessie said, "while there's still room in my little old brain for remembering how to walk."

They pushed out of the booth and headed for the door. Jessie was the last one out. Just before the door closed, she glanced back at Amory. He was standing behind the counter staring at her, his glasses halfway down his nose. She gave him a big, warm, friendly smile, and his expression brightened. He shoved the glasses up and smiled back at her.

"Hmmm," Jessie said, letting the door close behind her. "That might be goal number two."

"What?" Kate asked her.

"Nothing," Jessie said. "Just talking to myself."

Chapter 11

THE last thing Kate had said when they parted after the strategy session in the mall was, "I'll make up some excuse to call Mrs. Jesper and find out when she's coming this weekend. You can just happen to be there, too."

"Great," Jessie had said.

That had been last night. This morning it didn't seem so great. This morning the whole crazy idea seemed like something she'd need a fairy godmother for, rather than a family grandmother.

"Dad," Jessie said at breakfast before the younger children arrived at the table, "did you really mean it when you said I could use the money Gran gave you for Time-Out?"

"I meant it," her father told her. "What's more, I told Gran about it, and she's excited, too."

"She is?" Jessie said.

"You may not feel so happy about it when I tell you what she said." Her father was trying not to smile.

"What?" Jessie asked uneasily.

"She said she'd always wanted to learn to ride a horse." He laughed. "What with lessons for Sarah and lessons for Gran, you'll be lucky to have any time on the animal yourself."

"I'll manage. But don't let's say anything to Sarah about buying Time-Out. Not until we're sure," Jessie said.

"I may be slow on the uptake sometimes," her father answered, bending to drop a kiss on her head, "but some things I learn quickly. For example, never tell an eight-year-old anything that's not an accomplished fact." He paused a minute and patted Jessie's shoulder. "I can't tell you what it does for me to see you this happy," he said.

"If only Mrs. Jesper cooperates," Jessie said, her eyes shut tight on the hope. "We spent all of last night figuring out the best way to approach her."

"And what did you decide?"

The telephone rang before Jessie could answer him. It was Kate. "Saturday," she said when Jessie answered the phone. "I didn't even have to call her—she called here. She's bringing some men to see the colt, and she wanted to be sure we had him and Time-Out in the barn."

"What time?" Jessie asked, her stomach knotting up.

"Around two," Kate said.

Jessie hung up the phone and wiped her damp palms on the legs of her jeans. Her father was watching her. "Mrs. Jesper is going to be at the barn tomorrow at two. That's when I'm going to ask her," she said nervously.

"Whoever she is, she'll say no," Nick said, coming into the kitchen and sitting down at the table.

"Why do you say that?" Jessie asked.

"Because everybody always says no." As if to prove his point, he looked at his father and said, "Can I have a piece of last night's pizza for breakfast?"

"No," Mr. Robeson said.

"See," Nick told his sister. "I rest my case." And in spite of all her fears, Jessie had to laugh.

Saturday was one of those spring days that made you glad to be alive. The sky was a deep blue, so deep it almost looked fake. There wasn't a cloud anywhere.

Jessie and Kate were mucking out stalls. Dara was in the ring exercising Arpeggio. "I feel the way the pioneers must have felt waiting for the Indians to attack," Jessie said. She shoveled fresh bedding into the stripped stall, then stopped for a minute and looked at Kate. "What am I going to do if she says no?"

"She won't," Kate said.

"She might," Jessie insisted. "I have to accept that possibility."

"You're right," Kate said slowly. "You do."

"I really think it was better when I had no hope of ever owning Time-Out," Jessie said miserably. "Once you admit openly how much you want something, it hurts even more to think of not getting it."

"I guess that's true," Kate said, continuing to spread the new bedding with a rake. "But if you never try for what you want, you'll never have anything."

"Was that a car?" Jessie asked, sounding panicked.

"I think so," Kate answered. "Oh Jessie!"

Jessie dropped her shovel and ran to the door to look up the drive. Mrs. Jesper and a man were getting out of a car. "It's them!" Jessie said to Kate, her voice a tight whisper.

"Chill out," Kate whispered back. "Just remember all the things we told you. No matter what reason she comes up with for not wanting to sell Time-Out, you have a reason why she should."

Jessie nodded dumbly, her eyes glued to Kate's.

"And all you have to do is steer the conversation around to how much you enjoyed riding Time-Out last year, and what good care you took of her, and then mention how expensive it was for Dara to move Arpeggio here from Pennsylvania, and then . . ."

Jessie covered her ears. "I can't think anymore!" she said.

"Okay," Kate said quickly. "It's all in your head. It *is*," she insisted. "When you need it, it'll come. Do you want me to stay in here with you?"

"No," Jessie said. "I think I'd rather be alone with her." That way, if the worst happened, Jessie would have time to compose herself before she had to face her friend with the bad news.

They could hear Mrs. Jesper on the path, talking loudly and laughing with whoever it was she had with her. "I'd better get out," Kate said. "They'll be in here in a minute." She braced the rake against the side of the stall and held out her hands. "Give me five," she said, and when that was over she left the barn.

Jessie shivered. Outside she could hear Kate and Mrs. Jesper talking, and then Mrs. Jesper and her companion were walking toward her down the aisle.

"Hi, Jessie," Mrs. Jesper said. "We're here to give the colt another once-over. This is a friend of mine, Jim Richards. He trains racehorses."

"Are you going to race the colt?" Jessie asked, surprised.

"We're thinking of it," Mrs. Jesper said as they continued toward the back of the barn. "If Jim thinks he's got what it takes, that is."

Jessie could hear them talking together back there at Time-Out's stall. This is never going to work! she told herself despairingly. There was a slim possibility that Jessie could have carried off the girls' plan if Mrs. Jesper had been alone. But there was no way she was cool enough to take control of a conversation with two people—one of whom she had never seen before.

Jessie walked hesitantly to where they were standing at Time-Out's stall. The door was open, and Mrs. Jesper's friend had gone inside. Mrs. Jesper smiled when Jessie got to her and opened the door a little wider so that Jessie could see what was going on.

"Time-Out's not sure she likes this strange man getting familiar with her baby," Mrs. Jesper said. It was true. Time-Out's ears were pressed back, and she was holding her head low. "Maybe we should separate them," Mrs. Jesper said to her friend. "I'd hate to have you get bitten."

"She'll be okay," Jessie said, walking into the stall without even thinking about it. She stood in front of Time-Out and held on to her halter.

"He's a friend, sweetie," she said to the anxious mare. Time-Out's ears came forward, and she whinnied nervously. "He's not going to hurt your baby, I promise."

Time-Out nudged Jessie with her nose. "I think she feels better now," Jessie said to Mrs. Jesper. She held the mare, talking gently to her, while Jim Richards went over every inch of the colt.

"He's a beauty," he finally said. "I'd like a crack at training him."

"Really?" Mrs. Jesper said. She sounded thrilled.

"I think you might have a winner here. Look— let me show you. . . ."

Jessie wasn't sure if it was her imagination or not, but it seemed to her that the longer Mrs. Jesper and her friend talked about their plans for the colt, the more heavily Time-Out's head pressed against Jessie. She reached an arm over the mare's neck, laid her face against Time-Out's warm brown coat, and breathed deeply as if it were incense. Closing her eyes, she gave herself over to the love she felt for the quiet horse.

Jessie wasn't sure how long she and Time-Out stood there like that, but it dawned on her slowly that it was very still in the barn. She opened her eyes and looked behind her. Mrs. Jesper and Jim Richards were both watching her.

"You love Time-Out a lot, don't you?" Mrs. Jesper said softly.

Jessie nodded. Her heart was too full to speak for a minute. Then she swallowed hard and said thickly, "Mrs. Jesper, would you sell her to me?"

Mrs. Jesper looked at her a long time. Then she gave a deep sigh and glanced at Jim Richards, who smiled and shrugged.

"I guess you know we're moving," she said

finally to Jessie. "We had planned on taking the mare with us."

"I see," Jessie said, dropping her eyes. So it wasn't going to happen after all. . . .

"But maybe that isn't the best way to handle this."

Jessie's eyes lifted slowly. "Maybe it makes more sense to leave Time-Out here," Mrs. Jesper said. "After all"—she looked at Jim Richards—"it wasn't Time-Out's lineage that made the colt so special, it was his father's."

Jim nodded his agreement.

Jessie's head was spinning. Please, she kept saying over and over to herself. *Please.*

"I think we can work something out, Jessie," Mrs. Jesper said softly.

Jessie could never understand why she picked that moment to cry, but she did. She leaned her head against Time-Out's flank and cried so hard and long that she was ashamed of herself. And all through the tears, she kept saying, "I don't know why I'm doing this! I'm really happy."

When she had finally calmed down enough, she said, "Could my father call you tonight and make whatever arrangements are necessary?" she asked haltingly.

"That would be fine," Mrs. Jesper said. She hesitated a minute, then reached over to hug Jessie and kiss her on the cheek. "I'm happy for both of you," she said. "I'll talk to you soon." Jessie watched Mrs. Jesper and Jim walk away from her and out of the barn. Then she turned to Time-Out. "Did you hear that?" she asked, hardly able to believe it herself.

The mare caught the odd note in Jessie's voice.

She tensed, whinnied loudly, and eyed Jessie warily. "No," Jessie said, and laughed, "it's nothing to get upset about, it's good news. *Really* good news."

She turned suddenly and raced from the barn. "Kate! Dara!" she cried.

The two girls were in the ring and Jessie waited until they reached her—Kate on foot, Dara on Arpeggio.

They got to within a few feet of Jessie and stopped. Kate stared at Jessie, her eyes solemn. Then she came over and put her arms around her friend. "I'm sorry," she said. Stepping back, she offered Jessie a tissue. "If you feel like crying some more, go ahead."

As Jessie looked from Kate's solemn face to Dara's, she realized what she must look like. Her eyes were probably red and swollen and her face tear-streaked. No wonder the girls had gotten the wrong idea!

"I don't think I'll ever be sad enough to cry again," Jessie said, and watched as her friends' expressions slowly changed to disbelief.

"She said yes?" Kate gasped.

"She said yes!" Jessie cried, and both Dara and Kate whooped with joy.

Unsure what all this fuss was about, Arpeggio reared slightly and backed away. Dara turned him in a circle to quiet him down. "Isn't it a good thing we took the time to rehearse you?" she called over her shoulder. "How did you work the conversation around to selling her?"

"I used plan number three," Jessie said.

"Plan number three?" Dara asked in confusion. "Which one was that?"

"That was the one where I just stood there like

a dope and said, 'Mrs. Jesper, please, will you sell me Time-Out?' "

There was a pause while Kate and Dara digested the fact that Jessie hadn't used any of the help they'd given her.

Then Kate laughed. "That's the one I liked best, too," she said.

"Why?" Dara asked.

"Because that's the one that worked," Kate said, hugging Jessie again.

Chapter 12

JESSIE sat quietly on Time-Out's bare back. The mare grazed placidly, paying no attention to her passenger. Close by, the foal investigated the strange world of growing grass. In the exercise ring, which was separated by a rail fence from the field where Jessie sat, Kate and Dara were jumping Arpeggio and Night Owl.

Kate watched. "We'll be doing that soon," she said to Time-Out. The mare paid no attention to her. "It's going to take some work to get you back into shape. But we've got plenty of time. We'll work out a little when we have the ring to ourselves—and Chesapeake can watch." She looked over at the colt and tried to picture him at a racetrack, the name Chesapeake emblazoned on his saddle pad. As if sensing her interest, he stopped nosing the funny green things his mother was chewing on so blissfully and looked at her.

He had a fine head, and even in his young eyes, Jessie could sense some of the fire that Northern Spy's glance carried.

"I guess it's possible," she told the little animal.

"Jessie!" Kate called. "Watch this round and let us know what you think."

Jessie watched Kate and Night Owl go over the jumps, then Dara and Arpeggio. They were both clean rounds, and Jessie signaled that she could find no faults. It wasn't exactly the truth, though. Arpeggio's round had been crisper and more brilliant than Night Owl's, but Jessie wasn't going to tell Kate that.

Kate would find out soon enough, Jessie thought with a sigh. A few more times riding Northern Spy, and Kate would begin to realize on her own that he was a better horse for her needs than Night Owl.

Mrs. Wiley came out of the house, walking slowly—but walking without her crutches. She waved to Kate and then ducked under the fence to join Jessie and Time-Out in the field.

"Time-Out's looking good," Anne Wiley said.

"How soon do you think I can start working her a little?" Jessie asked.

"Maybe another week or so. You can ride her a bit here in the field. The colt will come right along with you, you know."

"I know," Jessie said, and laughed. She was thinking about the dream she'd had when first Sarah and then Kate had been riding Chesapeake.

Kate rode over to the fence. "Hi," she said to her mother.

"Don't come in here," her mother warned.

"I won't. Time-Out's a real pain about company."

"That's because the foal is still so young. She'll get over it," Anne Wiley answered.

"Jessie, Dara and I are going to take a trail ride.

Want to come?" asked Kate. "You can ride Night Owl, and I'll take the Spy."

"Great," Jessie said.

"You're invited, too," Kate said to her mother.

"Thanks," her mother said, "but I've got weeks before I can ride."

"At least you're not using crutches," Jessie said.

"Thank heaven for small favors," Mrs. Wiley answered, and laughed.

And big ones, Jessie thought, giving Time-Out a hug before slipping off her and heading for the stable after Kate.

The sun was warm on their backs as they left the farm behind and slipped into the shade of the woodland trails. Spy and Kate brought up the rear. It was safer that way. With Spy in the lead he had a tendency to set too fast a pace. Jessie could hear Kate laughing as Spy danced along. As usual, he was putting much too much effort into everything he did.

As Jessie posted to the Owl's easy trot, she thought she had never been happier in her whole life. "You know," she said half-turning in the saddle so Kate could hear her, "Mrs. Jesper said she had been thinking about offering me Time-Out even before I asked to buy her."

"I know," Kate said. "My mom said Mrs. Jesper heard you in the barn one day talking to Time-Out as if she were your best friend."

"She is," Jessie said. "Next to you and Dara," she hastened to add.

"Do you think she'd have sold you Time-Out anyway, without your asking?" Dara asked over her shoulder.

"No," Kate answered for Jessie.

"How do you know?" Jessie asked.

"Because Mom asked the same thing. Mrs. Jesper said she'd thought about it, then decided that it made more sense to keep the mare—until that day in the barn when you told her how much Time-Out meant to you, and she couldn't look you in the eye and say no."

"At least part of what we told you that night at the Lickety-Split paid off," Dara said.

"And just think—if you guys hadn't pushed me, it never would have happened."

"Not pushed," Kate corrected. "I'm sensitive about that word. We just pointed some things out, that's all."

"How about paying your dad back for your grandmother's money? Are you going to get a job?" Dara asked.

"Oh, I didn't tell you, did I?" Jessie said. "I've already got one."

"Doing what?" Kate asked. "Wait, let me guess. You're making sundaes with Amory!"

"No," Jessie said, and laughed, "but I have some news about that, too—remind me to tell you. As far as my job goes, remember I said that Mrs. Mac had to leave early two days a week? And my dad thought he'd have to replace her. Well, instead, I'm going to take her place. He's going to pay me what he would have paid her, and it'll work out fine."

"Not bad," Dara said, turning around to smile at Jessie. "I admire you for wanting to do that. Not everyone would."

"Jessica Claire Robeson would," Kate said airily. "She's one in a million."

They broke out of the woods into a long stretch of meadow that bordered a shallow stream. The girls had nicknamed the place the Racetrack because it was such an ideal spot to run the horses.

"Want to race?" Dara asked the other two.

"Sure," they answered.

They lined up, trying to get the horses even, and gave it up as impossible. When Dara called, "Ready, set, go," they took off at a dead run for the end of the meadow.

Night Owl moved easily under Jessie. She could feel the powerful thrust of his legs as they hit the ground. The wind whistled past her face, blowing her hair straight back from her head. They were covering ground at an amazing speed—but it was nothing compared to the speed Kate and Spy had achieved. In a matter of seconds they had left both Night Owl and Arpeggio behind.

At the end of the meadow, Spy came to a reluctant halt, and Kate circled him to absorb his leftover energy. By the time Dara and Jessie got to the end of the Racetrack, Kate was patting Spy's neck and laughing. "Are you okay?" Jessie asked.

"I'm fine," Kate said. "He is a devil, isn't he?"

"Almost," Jessie agreed wholeheartedly.

They walked the horses into the stream to let them drink a little, then entered the woods again at an easy trot. The newly budded leaves cast flickering shadows over them, and nest-building birds scolded as they passed underneath. The quiet and peace of the woods filled Jessie with so much contentment she almost couldn't stand it.

"Hey!" Kate said suddenly from her position behind Jessie. "What was that business about Amory? You said you had something to tell us?"

"Yeah," Dara said, reining in Arpeggio and turning to look at Jessie.

Jessie smiled smugly, first at Dara and then at Kate. "Amory and I are going to the movies Saturday night."

"You are?" Kate shouted. Startled, Spy reared slightly and danced around. "When did he call you?"

"He didn't. I was talking to him in the hall this afternoon, and I happened to mention that I wanted to see the film that's at the Playhouse. He said he did, too, and why didn't we go together Saturday night, so I said fine."

Dara looked at Kate and burst out laughing. "It's not funny, Cooper," Kate said in mock anger.

"Listen, Kate, the rest of the world is not going to sit around and wait for Pete to ask you out before it makes plans of its own," Dara said, and laughed again.

"Well, that's the final straw," Kate said. "The minute I get back to the house, I'm calling Pete and asking him if he wants to go out Saturday night."

"Maybe he'd like to double with Amory and me," Jessie said innocently. "It might give him some courage." That made Dara laugh even louder, and after a second Kate laughed, too.

"I guess that means this will be a short ride," Dara said, turning around and urging Arpeggio forward again.

"You lucky stiff," Jessie heard Kate mutter behind her. She had to smile. Luck hadn't had much to do with Amory's invitation. Being aware of Amory's interest, and being friendly to him, and just happening to be in the hallway at the same time he was, had had a lot to do with it.

Jessie was sure the reason Kate and Pete hadn't been out together yet was because Kate hadn't been ready. But from the muttering she could hear going on behind her, she bet that Kate was ready now.

She turned around and grinned at her friend, who grinned back at her. "You taught me all I know," she said to Kate, and meant it. There was just one more goal looming on the immediate horizon. Tonight her grandmother was having them for dinner, and Jessie had made up her mind to tell her how she felt about roast leg of lamb.

"I can't believe that for all my big talk, I'm such a wimp about asking Pete to go out with me," Kate said softly.

"Some things are harder to do than others," Jessie told her. "I myself face a major test tonight."

"Really?" Kate asked. "What?"

Jessie told her.

"Whew." Kate whistled. "Well, if you do that, Jessica Claire, I can call Pete."

"Is it a done deal?" Jessie asked with a grin.

"A done deal," Kate said.

GLOSSARY

BIT   A metal or rubber bar that is fit into the horse's mouth to help control the horse's direction and speed; part of the bridle..

BLAZE   A striking white marking of medium width that runs down the middle of a horse's face.

BREECHES   Riding pants, usually of a tight stretch material, that fit closely over the calves and are worn inside riding boots.

BROODMARE   Female horse used specifically for breeding.

BRIDLE   Headgear consisting of head and throat straps, bit, and reins. Used for controlling a horse.

CANTER   A rolling three-beat gait, faster than a trot.

CAVALLETTI   A series of long poles of adjustable height, supported by crossbars; used in teaching both horses and riders to jump.

CONFORMATION   A horse's proportionate shape or contour.

CRIB   A type of bin used to hold food for stable animals; "cribbing" is also a bad habit of horses who bite the edges of doors, feed bins, etc. while sucking in air.

CROSS-COUNTRY   A timed event that takes place on open land. These courses include riding across fields, through woods, and along trails, and require jumping over natural and man-made barriers such as ditches, logs, and hedges.

CROSS-TIES A pair of leads, one attached to the right side of the halter and one to the left, used for holding the horse in place while grooming.

CURRY To rub and clean a horse with a *curry comb,* which is a round rubber comb that loosens mud, dried sweat, and hair.

DIAGONAL In riding, refers to the rider's position at the posting trot as the horse moves diagonal pairs of legs. On a circle, the rider would be rising in the saddle as the horse's outside shoulder moves forward (and the inside shoulder moves back). This keeps the rider from interfering with the horse's balance and freedom of movement.

DRESSAGE Training a horse to perform with increased balance, suppleness, and obedience, and to perfect its paces. A dressage test involves a traditional system of complex maneuvers performed in an arena in front of one or more judges. The test is scored on each movement and on the overall impression that horse and rider make.

EVENT Also known as a *Horse Trail.* A competitive series of exercises which tests a horse's strength, obedience, and intelligence. Also used as a verb: "Now she has a horse of her own to ride and *event.*"

EVENTING Also known as *combined training* and *three-day eventing.* A series of tests combining dressage, jumping, and cross-country competitions.

FARRIER A person who shoes horses; a blacksmith.

FETLOCK The horse's ankle; a projection bearing a tuft of hair on the back of a horse's leg, above the hoof and the pastern.

FILLY A female horse less than four years of age.

FLANK On a horse, the fleshy part of the side between the ribs and the hip.

FOAL A horse under one year of age. Foals are usually weaned at six months and are then called weanlings. Also, to give birth to a horse.

FOALING BOX A structure used as a maternity ward for expectant mares, usually designed with a gap in the wall so that labor and birth may be observed secretly.

GAITS General term for all the foot movements of a horse: walk, trot, canter, or gallop.

GALLOP The horse's fastest gait, although there are gradations; an open gallop is faster than a hard gallop.

GELDING A male horse that has been castrated for the purpose of improving the animal's temper and health.

GIRTH A sturdy strap and buckle for securing the saddle.

GROOM To clean and care for an animal. Also the person who performs these tasks.

HALT In dressage, bringing the horse to an absolute stop with all four feet square and straight.

HALF-ALT A subtle signal that encourages the horse to gather himself, improving his balance and preparing him for a change of pace or direction.

HALTER A loose-fitting headgear with a noseband and head and throat straps to which a lead line may be attached.

HANDS A unit used to measure a horse's height, each hand equaling 4 inches. A horse is measured from the ground to his withers. Ponies stand up to 14 hands 2 inches (14½ hands high); larger horses are everything above. A 15-hand horse stands 5 feet high at his withers.

HAYRACK A rack for holding hay for feeding horses.

HOOF-PICK A piece of grooming equipment used to gently clean dirt and stones from between hoof and horseshoe.

IMPULSION The horse shows willingness to move freely, particularly through the powerful driving action of its hindquarters.

IN AND OUT Two fences positioned close to each other and related in distance, so that the horse must jump "in" over the first fence and "out" over the second.

JODHPURS Riding pants cut full through the hips and fitted closely from knee to ankle.

JUMPING In eventing, also known as *stadium jumping*. Horse and rider must take and clear ten to twelve fences in a ring. Penalty points are added for refusals, falls, and knockdowns.

LATERAL MOVEMENT When a horse moves sideways and forward at the same time.

LEAD The piece of rope or leather used to lead a horse.

LIPPIZANER A compact, handsome horse, usually gray, originally bred at the Lippiza Stud near Trieste; famous for their use in dressage exhibitions at the Spanish Riding School in Vienna.

MUCKING OUT To clear manure and soiled bedding from a horse stall.

OXER A jump or obstacle that requires the horse to jump width as well as height.

PADDOCK An enclosed outdoor area where horses are turned out and exercised.

PACE The speed at which a horse travels, or, in harness racing, a two-beat gait in which the legs on the same side of the horse move in unison.

PALOMINO Technically a color rather than a breed; a type of horse developed mainly in the southwestern United States. These animals have golden coats and flaxen or white manes and tails.

POST Rising up and down out of the saddle in rhythm with the horse's trot.

SADDLE FLAPS Side pieces on an English saddle. They hide the straps needed to keep the saddle in place.

SERPENTINE In dressage, a series of equal curves from one side of the ring's center line to the other. The horse changes the direction of his turn each time he passes over the center line.

SHOULDER A lateral movement in which the horse moves sideways and forward at the same time, bending his body around the rider's leg.

STANDARD An upright post used to support the rail of a hurdle.

STIRRUP LEATHER The strap used to suspend a stirrup from a saddle.

TACK The gear used to outfit a horse for riding, such as saddle, halter, and bridle.

TROT A two-beat gait faster than a walk, in which the horse's legs move in diagonal pairs (left forward, right rear).

WITHERS The ridge between a horse's shoulder bones. The highest point above the shoulders where the neck joins the back.

Here's a look at what's ahead in KATE'S CHALLENGE, the third book in Fawcett's "Blue Ribbon" series for GIRLS ONLY.

"Good morning, class," greeted Tommy Langwald, the combined training camp owner. "This morning we're going to concentrate on pacing—that is, knowing just how hard to push your horse around this tough course. I'm certain most of your horses can actually get over these jumps, but can you maintain a constant, accelerated pace? This is the real challenge and where you can lose a lot of points in competition. Okay, we'll go in the usual order."

Kate and Night Owl eyed the cross-country course eagerly. This was their favorite event of the three that made up the combined training regimen—dressage, cross-country, and stadium jumping. And Langwald's had a particularly beautiful course, the jumps following the natural roll of the land. From each rise was an intimate view into another section of the valley, not that you had time to ponder it when you were flying over three-foot obstacles.

Everyone watched as the first girl headed over the jumps. Kate held her breath. Horse and rider just weren't in sync. She could tell that the girl was giving signals that interrupted the horse's natural rhythm. He got over the jumps but he was always jumping too early or too late. Suddenly, at the water jump, the girl pulled back on the reins just as her horse took off. His balance was thrown off and he crashed into the planks before the water. Everyone gasped in horror as the rider flew over the horse's head.

"Roll!" yelled Langwald. "Keep rolling!"

She hit the ground and rolled over and over to get out of the way of the horse's hoofs and his body if he fell. Langwald ran over to her, but she was already on her feet. Grabbing her horse's reins without a word, the girl stomped off toward the barn.

"All right, class," said Langwald, returning to the group, "I think you can see the importance of pacing over these jumps. Let the horse tell you what to do. Feel it and go with him. Okay, Miss Wiley, you're up."

Kate shifted her weight forward and pressed the Owl's sides with her legs. Night Owl knew the signal and broke into a trot. More pressure from Kate and he switched smoothly into a canter. Kate urged him into the fastest pace she felt he could handle on this course and Night Owl responded. The first jump flowed by, and so did the next. They were connected. Then, at the next jump, a post and rails, Night Owl suddenly pulled out at the last minute. Kate was thrown to one side and just barely managed to stay on.

"Night Owl!" she whispered harshly, circling him back around. "What are you doing? Get yourself over this jump."

She headed him into it again, and again he pulled out.

"Hit him with your crop!" shouted Langwald. "He's playing games with you."

Kate glared at Langwald. She couldn't imagine striking Night Owl.

"Bird, get your buns over this jump," she said, and squeezed him into action with her legs. This time he slid to a halt right in front of the jump, and again Kate was almost unseated. Langwald was instantly beside her.

"If this were a trial, Wiley, you'd be disqualified. Three refusals and you're out. How does that make you feel?"

"I don't know what's wrong with him," said Kate, close to tears.

"Well, I do," barked Langwald. "He's not in the mood. These piddling little planks aren't challenging enough for him, so he's not going to do it. Get off him."

Kate didn't know what Langwald had in mind, but she dismounted. He took the reins from her and mounted Night Owl with a practiced ease. Kate watched in horror as he pulled his riding crop from his boot and whacked Night Owl soundly on the rump. Night Owl's ears shot forward and he pranced energetically. Langwald circled him and took him over the jump. He made it with a foot to spare.

"There," said Langwald, handing Night Owl back to Kate. "I think he understands who's in control now."

Speechless with anger, Kate took Night Owl from Langwald and stormed back to the group. Never had Night Owl been treated so roughly. It was unthinkable to Kate to use the crop on her beloved horse. She patted his neck comfortingly.

"Horses used for eventing, class, are not pets," said the man. "They are highly trained machines. Consistency is what you're looking for in them."

You're a highly trained machine, Kate raged inside. You wouldn't know a feeling or emotion if you tripped over it.

"Okay," continued Langwald, "class dismissed. Reconvene here at one o'clock. I think you could all use some extra work."